I THINK HE WANTS US TO MOVE

The comic exploits of a driving instructor

John Swift A.D.I.

Published by
THE OLD MUSEUM PRESS

I THINK HE WANTS US TO MOVE

First published by The Old Museum Press Limited
The Old Museum, Bramber, West Sussex BN44 3WE
England
1997

© John Swift 1997
All rights reserved

This book is sold subject to the condition that
it shall not, by way of trade or otherwise, be
lent, re-sold, hired out, or otherwise circulated
without the publisher's prior consent in any form
of binding or cover other than in which it is
published and without a similar condition
being imposed on the subsequent publisher.

A catalogue record of this book
is available from The British Library

ISBN 1 84042 016 2

Design, typesetting and format by StewART

Printed and bound in Great Britain by
Biddles Limited, Guildford & Kings Lynn

CONTENTS

Acknowledgements 5
Introduction 6

Chapter One
Getting Started and Watching out for the Cheapskates 8

Chapter Two
Keeping Matters Under (Dual) Control 16

Chapter Three
Key to a New Life 25

Chapter Four
Dangerous Liaisons 30

Chapter Five
Calm and not so Calm 46

Chapter Six
High Tech and Old Times 70

Chapter Seven
'L' is for Left 91

Chapter Eight
The Pleasures of Colditz 116

Chapter Nine
Frustration and Foreign Travel 132

Chapter Ten
Finally.......... 161

ACKNOWLEDGEMENTS

Cliff Gomersal A.D.I.
Mick Pearson A.D.I.
Bert Garlick A.D.I.
Mick Young A.D.I.
Eddie Seville A.D.I.
Andrew Walker A.D.I.
Phil Herring A.D.I.
Laurie Earle A.D.I.

and various other people who wish
to remain anonymous
........for a variety of reasons.

Thank you.

INTRODUCTION

Having spent the last 10 years as a Driving Instructor I have been privileged to teach quite a few people to become mobile. Many for the first time, others to change from two or three wheels to four.

During this time I have been privy to some euphoric highs and some really despondent lows. Whichever extreme my pupil of the moment was going through, I can honestly say, I felt the same.

Having now retired from active service, I have attempted to recall some of the numerous incidents that have occurred and record them in anecdotal form, I hope for the pleasure of others, whether they be drivers or not.

As I write, the driving instruction business is going through a hard time, mainly due to the fact that the Theory Test is tending to put people off taking lessons. This should not be the case, all instructors will provide help and tuition to pass the Theory Test. Books are also available to help in this direction.

Some of my pupils will identify themselves in the events related here but some names have been changed to protect the innocent. I am indebted to a number of instructors from the Leeds

Driving Instructors Association for stories they have passed to me. I also owe a debt to examiners who have been kind - or should that be cruel enough, to give me incidents to report.

While I'm expressing thanks to various people, let me offer apologies to lady instructors. It is not my wish nor intention to ignore their existence but I found it much easier to write using the male gender unless I was referring to specific incidents which involved ladies.

Chapter One
GETTING STARTED AND WATCHING OUT FOR CHEAPSKATES

We had just arrived home one Friday evening from our holiday in France when the phone rang. I picked it up and gave our number. A man asked, "Is that The John Swift Driving School?"

"Yes it is" I replied with as much alertness as I could muster after driving 590 miles and coming back to a doormat full of junk mail.

"I've got a driving test on Tuesday afternoon, will you take me for it?"

It was Friday and I don't usually work weekends in summer but we had just returned from an expensive holiday and anyway, business is business. As I reached for my appointment book, I asked him how many lessons he wanted over the weekend.

"Oh I don't want to book any lessons, I just want to take my test in a driving school car, I've failed three times in my brother's so I *can* drive"

I suppose I should have been used to similar requests and declined gracefully but I couldn't resist saying, "When you've passed your test and spent over 9000 quid on a new car and a complete stranger offers you £12 to allow him to take a driving test in it, what will you say?"

The reply came back without much thought, "I'd tell him to get lo - -"

The penny dropped as he completed his sentence.

"I couldn't have put it better," I said and went back to unloading the car.

·· 🕮 ··

Was I unreasonable? I don't think so, if I'd said 'yes', he may well have kept me on hold while he tried to find someone cheaper.

Fortunately it is only a small minority of the people who contact us who tend to abuse our services, although it can be said, the majority of the others, at times, abuse our vehicles but that's another story.

There are, at present, over 33,000 A.D.I.'s (Approved Driving Instructors) on a register maintained by the D.S.A. (Driving Standards Agency) the Government body which controls driver training and arranges driving tests.

To teach a complete beginner to drive and see them pass their test is a wonderful feeling and if ever that buzz goes out of the job, then so should the instructor. Passing their test is the aim of every pupil but that isn't all there is to driving and we have to think beyond the test to the future safety of everyone concerned when the open road beckons. In the words of the D.S.A - 'Safe driving for life' must be the objective of both pupil and instructor.

To qualify as an A.D.I. isn't easy. There are three examinations to be passed. A written exam is the first. One hundred multi-choice questions must be answered on the Highway Code and other motoring matters in 1 ½ hours in a classroom situation.

Next there is a one hour driving test under the strict gaze of a Supervising Examiner. Any more than six minor faults and it's a fail.

Finally, a further one hour test of instructional ability, during which the prospective A.D.I. must competently teach the Supervising Examiner two aspects of driving tuition, chosen at random by the examiner.

Once qualified and on the register, A.D.I.'s are subject to regular 'Check Tests' by the S.E.A.D.I. (Supervising Examiner for Approved Driving Instructors) during which the S.E. sits in the back of the instructor's car during a normal lesson and assesses whether his instructional ability is being maintained and that the A.D.I. is keeping abreast of any changes in teaching techniques.

Most A.D.I.'s start off working for a multi-car school which will supply both a car and pupils. This sounds ideal but of course this 'franchise' agreement means the school will expect a proportion of the A.D.I.'s earnings. Eventually as both experience and confidence grows, a lot of these A.D.I.'s will decide to go it alone. Some will do well and go on to run their own successful school, others will come unstuck.

There are millions of people spending many millions of pounds a year on driving lessons so how can an A.D.I. NOT succeed? All too simple. If they don't satisfy their pupils with the standard of their instruction then the pupils will leave - and it is very unlikely that they will recommend anyone else to go with that A.D.I.

Work dries up, mortgages and car loans are still to be paid and it becomes a very sad story.

A fully qualified A.D.I. will display a green 8 sided certificate in the bottom left corner of the windscreen. A 'Trainee' instructor will have a pink triangular certificate in the bottom left.

Trainees have still to pass the most difficult part of their examination, the dreaded Part Three. Having taken out a Trainee's Licence from the D.S.A., he should, by law, be accompanied and supervised by a qualified A.D.I. for 20% of the time he is working. When he feels sufficiently competent, he will apply to take his Part Three exam. At present a trainee can have three attempts to pass the exam, if he doesn't do so, then he would have to start all over again with Part One.

A loophole that I feel needs closing is the facility for multi-car schools to charge pupils the full lesson fee whilst providing them with a trainee instructor.

Having qualified and taken the plunge on his own, then an A.D.I. will have to supply his own car, find his own work and be responsible for his own book keeping and tax affairs. In there somewhere, are some very good reasons why some A.D.I.'s never take the step to leave the relative security of a school where they are looked after.

Whether an instructor starts off working for himself or someone else, the first few lessons are going to be as nerve racking for him as they are for his pupils, whose confidence would hardly be enhanced if they were aware of the situation.

Eventually the first test is reached. 'Pass' or 'Fail', it's a milestone in the A.D.I.'s career. My first two test candidates failed but I well remember the third. He passed and we made fools of ourselves by doing high fives in the middle of the main road.

If an A.D.I. is prepared to work over a large area, local press advertising is an option to find work and Yellow Pages will give the same wide coverage. Travelling over a wide area inevitably means a lot of 'dead time' moving between drop off and pick up points.

To avoid this scatter-gun approach to advertising, many A.D.I.'s place cards in local shops and Post Offices. Direct mail shots are another alternative. I had 1,000 leaflets printed and my wife and I delivered them around the area in which I wanted to work. I struck lucky and work came in in sufficient quantity to keep me going full time and from then on, I was able to rely on referrals.

Referrals are the most cost-effective way to get work. My area centred on a secondary school with a large sixth form which turned into a lucrative source of business. In return for all the work I was getting from the school, I offered to provide pre-driver training as part of their curriculum on a voluntary basis. Disappointingly I didn't receive a reply. A lot of schools are only too pleased to accept this kind of offer. Indeed, not so many years ago, A.D.I.'s were being paid to provide sixth formers with this sort of instruction.

For the most part, work will come via the telephone. A large proportion of this will, as time goes by, be referrals from satisfied pupils. Some of the calls though will be 'cold calls', i.e. potential pupils who have seen adverts or a phone number.

Referrals will be reasonably easy to convert into pupils, someone else has done most of the work for you but cold calls will require some effort to convert them.This is where telephone technique comes into play. It is well worth giving a lot of thought to this technique and working on it.

I discovered I didn't have THE worst telephone technique in the world when I was restructuring our front garden some time ago. I needed some top-soil and seeing an advert in the local freebie for 'Top-soil, £2 a bag' I called the number.

"'ELLOW" came a voice after a few rings.

"I'm enquiring about our ad for top-soil, what size are the bags please?"

"Abou' 'arfunderweight"

"I see, is it dry?" — pause,

'Why?"

"If it's dry, it'll be all soil. If you pack it after a thunderstorm, half of it will be water"

"You tak it as it comes"

So suitably impressed, I was encouraged to place an order. "I'll have one bag after a long dry spell and will you deliver it to 50 Rop-"

I just caught the words "P—- Off" as the phone went down.

Hardly appropriate in view of what I'd been trying to avoid!!

Driving lessons can be had for all sorts of prices and it would be too glib to suggest that you get what you pay for. Ask yourself however, "What level of PROFESSIONAL expertise can I expect from someone selling his services for less than £10 an hour these days?"

Starting up in business a new A.D.I., faced with existing competition may have to set low prices in order to break into the market and build a connection. What is worrying though is the number of A.D.I.'s who have been in the business many years, some of them up to 30, who are still finding it necessary to sell themselves cheaply. They are having to work many hours to make a reasonable living wage when they ought to be able to cut back on their hours. I'm not suggesting a cartel but in most countries in the E.U. a fair price is asked by all A.D.I.'s, the number of instructors is limited and a good living is available. The current policy of the D.S.A is not to limit the number of A.D.I.'s on the register thus making if virtually impossible for that situation to prevail in this country and therefore the status quo will go on and on.

As a back-up to the question posed in a previous paragraph, I offer the following incident.
At a time when the average lesson price was £10, a young man came to me having had four lessons at £3 an hour from another school. During those four lessons he estimated he had driven the car for no more than 1.½ hours. The rest of the time had been spent talking. They had talked about the Highway Code, about steering, gear changes, signalling, tyre pressures, loading the back seat when out shopping and the boot was full, the lot. Half way through the third lesson he'd been allowed to move the car. Mind you, it wasn't costing him a lot.....or was it?

No matter how much has been said about gear changing and no matter how many times it had been dry-runned, the pupil's brain appears to go to porridge the first time they try it on the move. I've found the quickest way for a pupil to pick it up, is to run through the various positions a couple of times and then practice gear changing while on the move. Most professional A.D.I.'s will have a pupil driving during the first lesson. It will depend on the capability of the pupil how far this movement is but even it if isn't far, it helps build confidence.

Chapter Two
KEEPING MATTERS UNDER (DUAL) CONTROL

There is a misconception that driving instructors require 'nerves of steel' to get through their working day, this isn't true at all. Safety revolves around having confidence and being in control. A.D.I.'s should be outwardly calm and showing they are in control ALL the time. It is the dual control system as well as ability that makes this possible. Duals are infinitely more use than a repeat prescription for Valium and should be the first piece of equipment fitted to a normal car to convert it to a driving school vehicle.

Most manufacturers are willing to do a deal regarding dual controls when one of their vehicles is purchased for tuition purposes. They will either supply or fit them free of charge and some manufacturers will even pay for both supply and fixing.

I remember driving a new car away from the showroom on one occasion after duals had been fitted. The first time I had to use my brake was just before I turned a sharp left hand corner shortly after leaving the showroom. As I took my foot off the brake I realised to my horror that the pedal had stayed down and I couldn't get round the corner until I'd hooked my foot under the pedal to lift it up. This moment of hesitation meant that I was going round the corner much slower than I would normally have done. It caused problems behind me. The van coming after me managed to slow down but the car behind the van didn't - and I heard the resultant bump.

Consequently, a small convoy of three vehicles trooped round the corner in slow motion. Even before we stopped, or so it seemed, two irate drivers descended upon me enquiring both as to my parentage and how I could call myself a driving instructor if I drove around corners in that manner.

My only defence was to get out and show them my brake pedal still on the floor where it had stayed when I braked to a stop. The same slow motion convoy then journeyed back to the showroom where the situation was explained to a red-faced manager and then to an even more red-faced technician who had failed to set the tension correctly on my dual brake.

The Company accepted full responsibility and I left the two drivers there to settle their insurance problems while I set off to pick up my next pupil after having my tensions re-set.

..🆔..

A faulty split-pin was the reason my dual brake let me down on another occasion.

Unknown to me, the split-pin somehow came loose and dropped out allowing the connecting rod that links the main brake pedal to my dual pedal to come adrift. I was testing my pupil's powers of observation at this particular point in the lesson.

"Take the next available road off on the left" was the instruction he was working to, with the accent on the word 'available'. The next turning on the left would be marked 'No Entry' and was therefore not available.

He missed the sign and started to turn in, having signalled late to do so. I squeezed my brake pedal, intending to bring the car to a stop, where he could see the 'No Entry' sign, but of course my brake didn't work because of the loose connection. I had to ask my pupil to stop the car by which time we were a couple of car lengths up this one-way street and that's rather an undignified place for a driving instructor to be. A case of the biter bit!!

○ ○ 🛇 ○ ○

An instructor shouldn't be constantly trampling on his dual controls, indeed his feet should be kept away from them unless he senses a problem. On today's busy roads there will often be the odd hairy moment, usually caused I have to say, by the impatience of other drivers.

How soon people forget that they were learners themselves - probably not so long ago. For too many drivers, a learner in front is either a problem or a challenge. The learner must be passed at all costs before the roundabout ahead. Why? What would it cost if they didn't? A few seconds? Not much more and certainly not enough to have to forego that G & T, but no.. FOOT DOWN — PULL OUT — GO ROUND — PULL IN — Phew!

It happens every day we are on the road. It may not be a roundabout, a driver may be waiting to come out of a junction, if our car wasn't displaying 'L' plates, he'd have waited but we are, so his foot goes down on the gas. As a consequence ours may have to go on the brake and too often sadly, he didn't consider there might be a vehicle close behind ours.

The biggest single cause of road traffic accidents is vehicles travelling too close to the one in front. So if he didn't look behind us before he pulled out, we may well have a problem that was not of our making, one vehicle pulling out in front and one too close behind leaves us with nowhere to go.

Constantly we find vehicles so close behind that they literally fill our rear view mirror. There is no need to be so near, it must give some drivers a perverse sense of pleasure to put the frighteners on learner drivers.

One girl said to me, "he's so close I can see his fillings"

She was one who didn't let it bother her but she was an exception. So if you are travelling behind a learner, don't be a nuisance, keep to a safe following distance and if you are coming out of a junction, look BEYOND the first vehicle which may be approaching.

A BMW driver who didn't show much patience finished up wishing he had.

I was 'with pupil' travelling down a main road, lovely day, not a care in the world, bills paid for another month, pupil doing very well, a shiny, new looking BMW purred up to the giveway lines a short distance ahead and to our right. He was indicating to turn to his right. I saw him glance at us and he should have waited but after a cursory look to his right, the gas went on and he seemed to squirt out of the junction into our path. A split second later he must have doubted his actions because he looked our way again, we were slowing down, we had to but the act of looking to his left must have affected his steering. The result was his near-side front wheel struck the high flinty kerb with a loud crunch. His tyre burst and I wouldn't be surprised if, judging by the noise, his wheel didn't suffer as well. I got out to see if he was all right. The window ~Zzzzzzzzed down as I came level with him and he growled,

"Why did you speed up when you saw I was coming out?" There didn't seem to be much I could do if that was going to be his attitude so I returned to my car and we resumed the lesson. He was on his mobile as we went passed and I couldn't resist saying to him…"Have a nice day now".

Dual controls are not compulsory on school cars but they are advisable if you want to leave the Grecian 2000 on the chemist's shelves. They go a long way to taking the stress out of the job for both instructor and pupil and, if they are honest about it, for examiners as well.

Everyone at times feels stress to some degree or other but being in control keeps it to a minimum. However there are one or two pupils who make even bomb disposal seem a better job alternative.

About a year after I qualified, I had a phone call from a lad who told me I had recently 'got a school pal of his through his test' and he wanted me to do the same for him. I made a mental note to tell him that we do not 'get people through their tests,' we teach them to drive properly and if they perform well enough on the day, they get themselves through their test.

He told me his friend's name was Roger and I remembered him as a pleasant, level headed 17 year old going on 21.

"Have you done any driving?" I asked. He had driven with both his parents and added,
"I'm a better driver than Roger"

"How do you know?"
"My mum says so"

I didn't let this glowing reference put me off. (I should have done) and arranged to pick him up at his home. His mum came to the door and told me her son was upstairs finishing his homework but 'should be finished' in about 10 minutes. While I twiddled my thumbs she threw in the juicy titbit that he had a test booked in three week's time but 'he'll only need 5 or 6 lessons' - quote..,
"We just want you to tell him what the examiners are looking for"!!

True to her word he was downstairs in about 10 minutes, no apology for keeping me waiting. (Never mind, it's coming off your lesson!)

We set off and he drove down their long, almost straight street, a little too quickly for my liking but no problems and after all he is used to this street. Into the main road, was that a sonic boom? The road was fairly traffic free but I pulled him in and made one or two suggestions that seemed appropriate, like 'take your time'!

Off again - he was a demon. No matter how many times I pulled him in over the next 10 minutes, he was off like the proverbial bat when he set off again. We probably only travelled 7 or 8 miles in 30 minutes, I stopped him so often. I discovered my car could go from 0 to 50 in under 9 seconds, I hadn't realised that before. I also found out I could bring it down to 0 again in about 3 seconds. I didn't like the smoke that came from the back wheels as I did this so I thought enough is enough and we headed back home. It didn't take us long to get there.

Both parents came out to see how he'd got on. I remember being surprised that neither of them mentioned we were back early. Usually when we meet parents they are on our side, after all they want their offspring to learn correctly and stay safe.

Working on this premise I expected a bit of backing from mum and dad. Not a bit of it, these two thought their little Sunbeam could do no wrong.

"I usually let him have his head for the first 20 minutes" said dad."If you'd done the same he'd have settled down"

This was in front of the kid, no reprimand for wasting time, his test was in three weeks and I've brought him back early on his first lesson with a flea in his ear.

"He drives us home from school most days and he does it perfectly" said mum helpfully.

How I let myself be talked into another lesson after that sort of logic I'm not sure, I must have needed the work. We arranged a time and as I was about to leave them, mum at her helpful best, gave me a parting shot,"maybe you won't be so picky next time!"

The evening before Sunbeam's next lesson I had a phone call from his mum. They had some shopping to do on their way home from school and would have to put the lesson back by 'about an hour.' She got a bit indignant when I told her I couldn't put it back because of other bookings.

"We'll have to cancel it then and arrange another time"

I pointed out that to cancel at such short notice would mean the lesson would have to be paid for. She immediately called off our beautiful friendship and challenged me to sue for the lesson charge. End of the Story? NO!

I didn't bother to sue but three years later, honestly, THREE YEARS LATER, I took a phone call from one of our local test centres telling me that a test I had booked for three day's hence would have to be cancelled owing to the examiner being ill.

I didn't have a test booked for that day so I asked for the candidate's name. It was Sunbeam. The test centre had tried to contact him but as he was unavailable they called me because I was listed on his application form as the driving school bringing him in for his test.

Later that day I called Sunbeam to pass on the message, his mother answered. I explained about the cancellation and got a right earful when I asked why my name was on his form, "It can't have been your name, my son is now with BSM and he is PROUD to be so"

I never did find out how or why I was listed as his instructor after all that time. I didn't even get the chance to ask if they'd slowed him down yet, she slammed the phone down on me. She didn't even have the good grace to thank me for not suing them for the cancelled lesson long, long ago.

End of the story? Not quite.

An interesting postscript came a few months later. I was in the test centre while a pupil was out on test. A BSM instructor, having seen my headboard as he came in, asked me if I remembered Sunbeam, he used his real name of course, funnily enough I did. He told me that he had passed his test a few weeks earlier. "But he was bloody hard work" he added.

Words had obviously passed between them about my connection, otherwise why would the A.D.I. have mentioned it. I'd love to know what was said but I was too proud to ask. It wouldn't have been good anyway, would it?

Actually I felt sorry for Sunbeam, not because it took him nearly 4 years to pass his test but for having idiot parents like those two.

End of story.

"Now we've found the accelerator, how about the brake?"

Chapter Three
KEY TO A NEW LIFE

Sunbeam's experience in taking a long time to pass his test is quite unique for a person who starts to drive at 17. It is not unusual for an older person to take a couple of years to do so.

I recall taking a phone call from a lady asking if I would give lessons to her daughter. The note of trepidation in her voice made me curious so I asked if her daughter had done any driving previously, "Yes, she has had three lessons but she didn't get on with her instructor"

All A.D.I.'s will have heard something like this from potential pupils and although it may well be the case, it is usually a euphemism for 'It wasn't as easy as she expected it would be'

It turned out to be a bit of both.

The daughter was in her mid 30's with no aptitude for driving at all. She had no co-ordination twixt hands and feet whatsoever. I was in fact her third instructor. After her first lesson, the instructor had, in effect, asked her not to call him, he would call her. After two weeks had passed she realised he had no intention of doing so. The second A.D.I. didn't show up for her third lesson with him.

On our first lesson together she told me she was determined to learn and as she had been so badly treated by her other two 'professional' instructors, I was determined to teach her. We had lessons twice a week, almost every week for nearly two years. Jayne passed her test at the third attempt. After the first two tests she was quite alright even though she failed but when she passed, she was in floods of tears throughout the journey home.

She composed herself before getting out of the car and as she did so Jayne revealed where her motivation for all the hard work had come from, "I've been wanting to leave my husband for three years. This is the first real thing I've done on my own and I'm hoping it will give me the confidence to get away from him".

A week or so later, I had a note from her, thanking me and saying that passing her test had already changed her life. I don't suppose, on reflection, it's the first marriage an A.D.I. will have broken up.

Not all courses end on a happy note. I gave a young man some lessons in exchange for some double glazing work. A driving licence would enable him to get more work by being able to travel further afield.

Two weeks after passing his test he lost his licence because of a bout of drinking and driving. Stupid boy.

Another bit of stupidity came about as the result of a boy I was teaching asking if I would give lessons to his older brother. It turned out that big brother had only recently returned home after a stint at Her Majesty's pleasure. He'd been 'sent down' for car theft and so-called joy-riding.

Apart from a few careless habits, crossing hands, late braking and doing 65 on a 30mph dual carriageway, he was quite a good driver. His gear changing was good, mirror work spot on and he knew where to position the vehicle. He had 7 lessons and passed his test.
Three weeks later, I saw him being picked up by the police during a televised drug swoop.

A driving licence can open up job opportunities, so it must be worth making an effort to keep it. The lad in the preceding paragraph, having already been in jail, had a chance to advance himself. Unfortunately he was foolish and shot himself in the foot by getting into trouble again.

Another example of shooting your own foot off came by way of a video to A.D.I.'s from the D.S.A. For many years a disturbing fact has been the number of drivers involved in road traffic accidents soon after passing their test. In an effort to cut down on this number, the D.S.A introduced the 'PASS PLUS' initiative. This would involve new drivers taking 6 post-test lessons with their instructor. Each one being an extension, not a repetition, of previous lessons, the exception being a motorway session.

Pupils would not be tested but would have to drive sufficiently well to justify their A.D.I. signing a form to that effect. This would then be sent to the D.S.A. who would then issue a certificate to the pupil that would entitle them to a substantial discount from their insurance premium.

The initial reaction to Pass Plus was not as good as had been anticipated, despite the cost of the extra lessons being more than adequately covered by savings on insurance. In order to stimulate interest in the scheme, the D.S.A produced a video that A.D.I's would loan to pupils, hoping to whet their appetite for Pass Plus lessons. The D.S.A are always stressing to A.D.I.'s the need to be professional in their outlook and behaviour. However they shot themselves in BOTH feet with this video.

It showed a scruffy looking instructor dropping a pupil off after a lesson, on the left hand side of the road. As he pulled away from the kerb he crossed his left hand over on the steering wheel so that both hands were pulling the wheel down on the same side.

Whatever happened to 'push and pull?'

Worse was to follow. As he moved away from the kerb, we saw an advert on his car door for *'Driving Lessons £6.99 per hour'* What's wrong with that? The average price for lessons at that particular time was £13 to £14. How professional can you be?

All the videos had to be returned and subsequently replaced, after all, what A.D.I. charging a realistic price was going to use *that* in an effort to promote Pass Plus? I shudder to think how much that cost the D.S.A and I can't help wondering what job the person responsible was promoted to.

When the D.S.A introduced Reverse Parking into the driving test they opened up a new can of worms. Prior to its introduction, EVERY instructor professed to teach the manoeuvre as part of their course. If this HAD been the case, I feel we wouldn't have seen such strange reactions from car owners as we did.

The manoeuvre involves pulling up alongside another vehicle and reversing into a parked position within two car lengths of the object vehicle.

If this sort of thing had been going on for years, why then did we see so many protective car owners appearing alongside us as we performed the manoeuvre? Drivers would come out of houses and remonstrate with us. Some even moved cars down the street, up the street and in some cases to the other side of the street. The larger ones among them had a very nasty tendency to lean on and rock our vehicles - the men were just as bad! Words would be exchanged, we'd explain, "just doing my job guv."

"Well don't do it near my car, I've just washed it"

Why they felt their cars were in jeopardy, I've no idea. One poor A.D.I. had a bucket of cold water thrown over him. He could only console himself, as he sat there with water trickling down to his toes, that it could have been something much worse than cold water. He told me that he would have got out and done some retaliating but the water bearer was Giant Haystacks in drag.

The situation has settled down a bit now and if we do get requests not to perform around certain vehicles, we'd respect it (I think). The half drowned one has now left the industry and taken up something less violent.

Chapter Four
DANGEROUS LIAISONS

On one occasion, a different type of problem manifested itself in Leeds. AD.I.'s cars were coming in for some dangerous aggravation on a particular estate. Gangs of youths took to surrounding school cars and making it difficult to drive away. This went on for a couple of weeks and culminated in two serious occurrences.

Not content with surrounding and rocking a car while a lady instructor was briefing a girl pupil, the yobs tried to get into the car. The instructor, by shouting to her pupil to give it some gas was able to get away using her dual controls. The second incident involved a brick being thrown through the rear window of an instructor's car from a moving vehicle. Both these incidents were reported to the police but there was little they could do.

As instructors we could of course stay away from the estate during teaching and this we did as soon as word got round. The L.D.I.A. (Leeds Driving Instructors Association) wrote to the examiners asking them not to take our cars onto the estate on test. This request was acted upon immediately and the test route involving the estate wasn't used until the estate got rid of the problem.

We are sometimes a bit vulnerable but we do learn where it is safe to take pupils and where not. Quite a few colleagues have had other scares while working but fortunately not many have ended badly.

An incident I was involved in could have been nasty but actually ended up with a good laugh.

Just before dusk, a pupil was starting a turn-in-the-road manoeuvre, she'd got about half way across the road on the first element when an old Ford Escort shot out of a junction to our left. It raced towards us, stopping less than a couple of metres away from my side of the car. Within seconds, the Escort looked like a cattle truck, three heads stuck out of three windows and started hurling abuse at us. Long gone are the days when I would have considered getting out of the car and slapping them with my handbag, so I resorted to taking my pen from it's permanent resting place, behind my ear and looked down at the Escort's number plate. I had to look down - it was so close to me.

As I started to write the number down - I don't know what I was going to do with it - it just seemed a good idea at the time, the driver slammed into reverse and executed a nifty two-point turn and shot off down the road. As he left us I noticed that the rear number plate was different to the one I'd just written down – strange!

I apologised to Emily for the atrocious language we'd been subjected to. She was a quiet girl from a good family so it came as a surprise when she said, "Oh don't worry about it, it was just like a school sports day".

Our driving test may not be perfect but from what I've heard of other country's efforts, it appears to be as good as any and far better than most.

An examiner in Leeds favoured Texas for his holidays. On his third visit he thought it would be interesting to take a driving test there. In Texas it isn't necessary to book a test, you simply drive up and wait your turn. He passed the theory test and as his turn for the practical came he was approached by a large uniformed policewoman, complete with holstered gun at her hip. She was to be his examiner, as in Texas it falls to the police to do driver testing.

He got in his car with her and followed her directions which included helpful warnings about heavy traffic. A couple of times around the block in his hired car, back into the car park and he'd passed his test.While the policewoman was filling in his details, she asked him what he did in the UK. "I do the same job you've just done but I don't need a bloody great gun to do it"

.. 🛇 ..

Vanessa came to me for lessons holding licences she had obtained in Kenya and Laos. Neither are valid in this country - I can't think why!!Her Kenyan licence was accepted in Laos so why not here? After all she had taken a three part test in Kenya.

Part One involved moving Dinky toys around on a ply-wood mock up of a 4 lane highway. She had to demonstrate correct positioning at half a dozen junctions on the board. No pressure and plenty of time to consider. To make the situation seem more bizarre, there were no 4 lane highways in Kenya.

Part Two was about road signs. She had to identify two and one of those showed an elephant in the road. She knew that because it said 'Elephant in the road'.

Part Three - now came the crunch. She was expected to drive the examiner's pick-up truck a full 30 metres along a straight but dusty road. As if that wasn't hard enough the rotten examiner had put a dust-bin in the middle of the road for her to avoid.

While she drove, three other test candidates squatted in the back of the truck awaiting their turn, so she didn't even have to drive it back, someone else did that while she took her place in the back of the truck. Incidentally the examiner turned it round at the end of each test.

Prior to taking her test Vanessa had hired an instructor who, on payment of an extra £5 had guaranteed that she would pass her test first time. He's not much of a gambler is he?

·· 🗋 ··

Not all OUR instructors are beyond reproach. One pupil told me he had been abandoned by a previous instructor at a fairly remote spot he'd been taken to for his first lesson. He'd not been charged for the lesson but when the A.D.I. had seen how he couldn't control the clutch pedal, he'd turfed him out with the words, "I think too much of my car to let you loose on it".

A lady in her 50's who managed a nursing home, told her employers she had been offered a similar job nearer home and would like to take it. She didn't drive and her present place of work was a bit difficult for her to get to. In order to keep her, her current employer offered her a company car if she could pass her test.

Their son was a driving instructor and he was lined up to give her some lessons which the lady herself would pay for. These lessons went on for quite some time. A friend of hers asked me if I would assess her progress because the lady felt she was being held back.

I don't think any A.D.I. would particularly relish this type of request, it is asking you to comment on someone else's professionalism. However I did it and felt she had a genuine grievance, despite being new to my car she performed very well.

I suggested she ask her instructor to put her in for her test. She called me and said he had flatly refused saying she wasn't ready. She asked me to take over her lessons, she passed her driving test within 4 weeks having had 7 lessons in my car.

I received another call from her a week later saying her employers had withdrawn their offer of a company car. She was understandably upset, it seems they had used the car as bait to tempt her to stay, feeling she wouldn't qualify for it.

Having passed up on the other job and not looked for another in the meantime, her employers had kept her with them for another year. She was considerably out of pocket and she couldn't afford to buy her own car and left her job on principle.

An A.D.I. called me one evening to ask me to teach his daughter. In answer to the obvious question, he just said, "We've had a bit of a row"

Arrangements were made and when I picked her up she told me she had had 4 lessons from her dad and each one had ended up as a slanging match. I'd heard her dad had a bit of a reputation for shouting at pupils occasionally but he'd always been in work, so I found it hard to believe. Tina confirmed it but before long I found *she* was shouting at *me* if things didn't go quite right. The hard word was issued but she definitely had a dodgy temperament and it couldn't go on. She wouldn't settle down so I gave her the heave-ho.

I still see her dad and it seems like an unwritten law, we never mention Tina. He's still working as he has done for nearly 30 years so his shouting can't be all that bad. I reckon it's that Tina but I'll never find out.

We hear many weird and wonderful excuses for failing tests -

"I've never driven behind a horse-box before" one pupil told me.

"I saw a schoolfriend and thought she was going to wave to me"

"Some of those questions are not in my copy of the Highway Code"

"I think I got a bit close to the vehicle in front 'cos he said to me, 'Do we need the headlights on under this lorry?'"

"He said I should have used the bus lane but no-one else did"

"I joined a funeral procession and it didn't seem right to overtake"

"That wasn't a one-way street last week".

"This is a one way street you know."
"But I only want to go one way."

I think my favourite came from John, a lad who actually lived on the street where he was asked to perform his emergency stop. The examiner had briefed him that the stop was due at any time. John was driving along, his speed was good for the conditions, then he saw his dad coming out of their garden gate. His dad recognised my car and waved to John. Just at that moment the signal came to STOP.

John being distracted, slammed the brake on. Even in an emergency the braking should be controlled and not whacked on as John had done. It might not have been quite so bad but the day before, the street had been re-surfaced and to quote John, "We must have slid about half a mile on the loose shale." He did explain about his dad to the examiner and although he was sympathetic, he had to give John the thumbs down.

Between lessons one morning I was taking a tyre to be repaired. I use a tyre specialist who will repair punctures while I wait, a useful service for A.D.I.'s and taxi drivers who cannot afford to be without a spare for too long. His shop is alongside a number of small garages and paint shops.

Going down the street passed the garages I saw George. George is getting on a bit, he's a quiet, nearly retired A.D.I.. He was being harangued by a large mechanic from one of the garages and looking very worried. I stopped opposite the scene and wound my window down. As mean as I could, I called, "Are you alright George?"

The menacing mechanic glowered at me and shouted, "What are you going to do about it if he's not?"

By now I'd had a closer look at George and said with some relief, "Nothing, it's not George".

I taught a tiny nurse to drive and after she passed she asked me to give lessons to her boyfriend (driving lessons) Susan was about 5' tall but Alan seemed to be about 6'10". I had a Renault 5 at the time, it's quite a small car and Alan's head was pressed against the roof. If I'd had a sunroof he'd have been sticking out of it.

It simply wasn't safe for him to drive like that, so I passed him on to a friend with a bigger car and resolved to get a larger car myself as soon as possible. I saw the two of them out shopping a few times and the difference in size was so marked, it was impossible not to wonder how ... but that's nothing to do with me .... or you!

An examiner told me of a time when he was working in Aberdeen. A colleague of his had a young man out on test on a very windy day. The instructor had opened the sun-roof on the way to the test centre, despite it being windy, it was very warm in the car. He had decided to leave it open during the test for the comfort of both examiner and pupil.

After a while, because of the wind noise, the candidate was having a degree of difficulty hearing the examiner's directions. A mite exasperated at having to repeat himself so often, the examiner reached up and tugged the sun-roof shut. A few moments later he asked the driver to park up on the left and asked him for a turn-in-the-road manoeuvre. The candidate did the manoeuvre reasonably well but the examiner wasn't satisfied with his observations. Nor was he happy with them at a subsequent reverse manoeuvre. Back at the test centre, he completed the Highway Code section and then told the boy that his driving had not reached the required standard. It was mainly his observation that had let him down, he said.

The examiner then got out of the car and the boy reached up and opened the sun-roof thus releasing his hair which had become trapped when the examiner had slammed it shut.

.. 🛍 ..

The Scots boy should have told the examiner his hair was caught immediately it happened, that is plainly obvious but it isn't always easy to do the obvious when under strain. Most people would have reacted differently, it was in this lad's nature to say nothing unfortunately.

How you are going to react to a situation will depend largely on your character. Some people are cool under pressure, others are volatile and some, to put it bluntly, don't have a clue what to do.

We see all types of personality characteristics in driving instruction. Something untoward happens and even pupils who are apparently test ready react differently. To some the unexpected is a challenge, to others it can have them contributing handsomely to my swear box. It is the last group that we have to sort out, the ones who could go to pieces if things don't go smoothly.

There are moments on lessons which I call 'Pure Gold'. No matter how many times I tell a pupil to wait for a left signalling vehicle to start turning in, before we emerge into it's path, they are likely to forget but if we're on lessons and that vehicle doesn't turn in but comes straight on, then they will always remember it.

Two people with totally different characters were Anne and Sarah. Neither of them were from Leeds but they were flat sharing students at Leeds University. They started lessons at the same time, both having one lesson a week. Anne was brash and confident while Sarah was a bit shy and nervy. Anne questioned everything we did but it was difficult to get Sarah to do more than answer my questions.

Anne was test ready about three weeks before Sarah but she went to pieces on test and failed miserably. She was to fail a second time but passed at her third attempt. Quiet Sarah passed first time nearly two months ahead of her flat mate. Anne didn't change but I could see Sarah getting more confident and more talkative in those two months I was picking Anne up. I don't think anything would change Anne's outlook on life but passing the test first, certainly brought her friend out of her shell - and must have stood her in good stead for anything else she tackled in life.

I came across yet another type of temperament shortly after getting my larger car. A phone caller asked me how tall I am. I'm just over 6' and when I told him he said, "Are you comfortable in your car?"

"Yes, why do you ask?"

"I'm 6'4 and I can't fit into a lot of cars, do you think I'll be alright in yours?"

I offered to take it round and let him try it out. He felt alright so I started giving him lessons. Not only was he 6'4 but was burly with it. Terry was a gas fitter and he felt he needed to drive urgently. His company had dropped hints that if fitters couldn't drive themselves to jobs it might be difficult to keep them on. He had lessons two and three times a week and made good progress. A couple of mock tests were completed satisfactorily and test day arrived. His test was at 9.30 am, I arrived to pick him up at 8.20. He lived with his mother and it was she who answered the knock.

"Sorry love, Terry isn't here"

"Where is he, can I go pick him up?"

"No, he didn't sleep at all last night and he left early this morning to avoid seeing you. He couldn't face his test but he's left your money".

6'4 and built like a brick sh.....ed and he couldn't face his driving test! Even so, I'd like him on my side in a scrap.
He did ring me about 5 weeks later to apologise and say he'd like to have another go. He had a couple of lessons but his heart wasn't in it and I wasn't surprised when he called it a day. I don't know what happened about his job.

￮￮🗲￮￮

Another 6 footer, this time a girl. Donna was a nurse and her legs seemed to go right up to her ears. She didn't wear skirts she wore pelmets. Donna passed her test at the second attempt and as I walked past the examiner in the street he smiled and said, "I'll bet you're sorry to lose her as a pupil".

Here I was, all this time thinking they didn't notice things like that!

An examiner told me of the occasion he had a very glamorous middle aged lady on test. It was a very warm day and the front windows were down to get some air into the car. The candidate was waiting in a side road for traffic lights to change, when a large Labrador dog made them both jump, as it put it's front paws on the window ledge at the driver's side and proceeded to lick the make-up off the lady's face. They managed to get rid of the dog and carried on with the test, which the lady finished rather less glamorous than she started.

Unlike most professional bodies where practitioners have to prove themselves capable by passing examinations, A.D.I.'s have to suffer the indignity of having on-going tests of their ability. So long as doctors, lawyers, undertakers and the like keep up to date with changes in their professions and no-one lodges a complaint against them, then they are free to pursue their chosen career as long as they see fit, without outside interference. Not so driving instructors.

These on-going bouts of delight are 'Check Tests". They are to an instructor what a visit to the dentist is to a 7 year old child.

Because, one hopes, they don't occur very often, it is difficult to get used to them. Rather like filling in an annual tax return, if you did it every week, it would be a simple formality but once a year makes it almost a new experience every time.

If an A.D.I.'s teaching falls below standard during the check lesson, then he will be given a Grading from one to three. These marks constitute a fail. At present he will be given two more opportunities to obtain a Grading from 4 to 6. Grade 4 is the lowest pass mark and would necessitate another check test within a year. Grades 5 and 6 would have to forego the pleasures of another check for three to four years. Should an A.D.I. fail to reach Grade 4 on his three tests then he would be removed from the register and lose his livelihood.

Better brains than mine have been wracked over the years to find a fair and adequate way to test an A.D.I.'s on-going teaching skills. Is there any need for it?

Many times the D.S.A have admitted that a Check Test is not and can never be a true reflection of an instructor's ability. He is being watched for one lesson out of many hundreds he will give over a year. There will be some nerveless ones among the fraternity but to the vast majority of A.D.I'S a Check Test is anathema.

It sounds easy to accept the suggestion from others to simply 'be yourself' and give a normal lesson. Many A.D.I.'s have told me that they found themselves giving instructions where it wasn't necessary. As soon as they had spoken the words they realised they wouldn't have done it normally as the pupil didn't need instructions at that particular moment - but it's too late, the words are out. At the end of the lesson, they've been marked down for over-instruction.

We have been told by S.E.A.D.I.'s that should a driving school show evidence of recurring faults, causing pupils to fail tests, or incur a preponderance of certain minor faults, then the instructor concerned would be asked to attend the S.E.'s office to discuss the apparent problem and if necessary a Check Test could follow.

There is a procedure in force including the necessary form to implement this control. Why cannot this procedure be enlarged upon and make regular Check Testing obsolete?

During a period when I was very short of morning pupils, I had a Check Test due at 9.30 a.m. The only pupil I had available on that day at that time was Annie who had been away for a week on a University Geology trip.

She had wanted to give the trip a miss because she had her driving test booked for two days after my Check Test. Her Prof. had dictated that she attend and this meant missing out on two lessons at, for her, a critical time. She was due back in Leeds the evening before my session with 'Torquemada'.

To make sure everything was in order, I phoned Annie's flat only to be told she wasn't getting back until three in the morning. As a precaution I put my wife on stand by – after all, she'd promised for 'better for worse'. Annie's flatmate said not to worry, Annie was an early riser and she was sure it would be alright.

It was, I picked her up at 8.30. I could tell she hadn't unpacked her bags yet, they were in evidence under her eyes.

I briefed the S.E. about Annie and explained our intentions and we set off.

Apart from her emergency stop, I thought she did quite well considering she'd missed her last two lessons, had hardly any sleep and had a strange bod in the car. The emergency stop was a bit lengthy, in fact, as I recall, after giving her the signal, I'd got time to say, "make it today, won't you".

Afterwards she told me she was afraid to stop too quickly, "In case your friend in the back wasn't ready, he seemed to be looking out of the window!"

We got back to the test centre, he gave me my mark, I kissed his feet and he said, "I don't think Annie is ready for her test yet" At the start of the lesson I'd told him she had her test later in the week.

Annie and I squeezed another lesson in the next day and she passed her test the day after. She told me the experience of having the S.E. in the car on *my* test had helped her with hers.

.. 🗓 ..

I've always found driving instruction to be very long on coincidence. In 10 years I've only had three pupils called Jenny and they were all learning at the same time. A man called Sam called me for lessons, 4 days later Samantha rang me and started, no Sams, before or since. Lots of little quirky coincidences like that.

Another area for coincidences is the *time* pupils want lessons. During some periods pupils are falling over themselves for morning lessons, other periods, evenings will be favourite. Lunchtimes are always popular. This crowding makes it difficult to fit people in sometimes. Often a person will start off by saying, "I can ONLY have lessons at such and such a time" but by the time we've sorted ourselves out it could be a totally different time we settle on.

Nurses work peculiar hours and often don't know what shift they are working from one week to the next and they take some sorting out.

Alison was a nurse and for her test she got a new examiner on his first day at my local test centre. She passed and I dropped her at work afterwards.

When I got home during the afternoon, my wife told me I had to ring our new examiner at the test centre. He was young, Alison was a bit of alright, so, I thought, 'Ello'ello.' No, nothing like that. It transpired that he hadn't filled Alison's pass certificate in correctly. He'd not filled in the category of vehicle she'd taken her test in.

"Can you get it back for me?" he wanted to know.

So I put down Cupid's bow and said I'd see if she would part with it that evening. I was due up at the test centre next morning so I told him I'd drop it off.

"Can you do it quietly?"

I knew what he meant. We had at the time an obnoxious Senior Examiner in charge there. It was done, the certificate was amended and returned to Alison.

Although he said how grateful he was, he still knocked back the next pupil of mine he took for test. Some people don't seem to know what gratitude means do they?

Chapter Five
CALM AND NOT SO CALM

I suppose it's the same all over but Leeds City Council have been going barmy constructing traffic calming zones. Some of them are very useful sensible requirements but others appear to be playgrounds for 'joy riders'. They love to zip in and out of the piers built out from the kerb. These piers are meant to slow drivers down in an effort to keep people alive, some chance the way some of the kids bomb around. Half the time the car has been stolen so they don't care how much damage they cause and if they get caught there is little the courts can do if they are under age. These kids are committing adult crimes so they should be treated as adults when it comes to punishment.

Two A.D.I. friends of mine had their cars stolen, one of them had only had his back three days and it went again. It finally put him out of business. He became demoralised. The second time it went missing, the thieves set fire to the seats and ruined the interior. Obviously he was insured but that only covered his vehicle and not his spirit.

A Jewish boy I was teaching had a weird sense of humour. He kept on telling me Jewish jokes, some of which I understood but others he had to explain. Our lesson was taking us through one of these 'calmed' junctions. He was a bit hesitant as we came to the second set of traffic lights having passed the first on green. I urged him to keep going and when he hesitated again coming to the third set, I told him the lights were *synchronised* in our favour. He screwed his face up and squeezed his legs together and said, "don't say that word to a Jewish boy." He was nearly 18, surely he can't remember that far back or could it be dyslexia?

It had been a long day, made even longer by that horrible intermittent rain which had meant the wipers being put on and off every few minutes.I got home about 8.30 just as my wife was taking a lamb casserole out of the oven, bang on cue. I went to the bathroom to ablute and the phone rang, (no silly, not in the bathroom.)

Kath answered it and called me saying it was an enquiry. Thinking she would have told them who they had got through to, I just said, "Hello."

A man's voice asked, "Is that" - - his voice tailed off, I think he was looking at a list,
"John Swift's Driving School?"

"Yes"

"How much do you charge for lessons?" the voice DEMANDED.

I told him.

"Bloody hell, they're getting dearer Janice. Listen, my son's 17 and bright, how many lessons will he need to pass his test, he's driven a lot with me?"
Now I should have been gentler with him - but he was

swearing, I was hungry and my lamb casserole was on the table waiting.

"What's my middle name?" I asked,

"What? How do I know, what sort of stupid question is that?"

"Well you asked me one so I thought I'd ask ...."

Can't they sound abusive on the phone some people?

Anyway, I probably asked for his retort, so I took some of his advice and got stuffed into my casserole.

..🕮..

The length of waiting time, to get an appointment for a driving test, will vary up and down the country. If things are working smoothly, the appointment would be made by the D.S.A. about 4 to 5 weeks after the application was received by the booking office. This length of time would satisfy the D.S.A. and most instructors would be happy with it so long as it doesn't fluctuate too much and too often.

It is no use waiting for a pupil to become test ready before applying, as this would keep them either hanging on doing lessons they don't need or not driving during the waiting time. This means the crystal ball has to come into use in order to time things correctly.

Using professional judgement, A.D.I.'s can usually get the date about right. Occasionally though, things can go wrong. The weather, illness or a change in working conditions can throw a spanner in the works. If a pupil has to miss lessons, for whatever reason, or doesn't make the expected progress and it becomes clear that they are not going to be ready in time, then a decision has to be made in order to give the D.S.A. 10 CLEAR WORKING DAYS notice of either postponement or cancellation, otherwise the test fee is forfeit.

If something occurs within the 10 clear days to make it unlikely that the pupil will be ready for test, then we have a problem. Unless extra time can be found, by both pupil and instructor, to raise driving standards, then we must look very seriously at not allowing the test to go ahead. This action will give no-one any satisfaction but if we feel the pupil is not capable of driving safely then we must withdraw the use of our vehicle. All sensible A.D.I.'s will have this facility written into their terms and conditions.

We cannot prevent anyone taking a test but this action is our final attempt to stop the pupil putting themselves and others involved in danger. If they should decide to go ahead in another vehicle, then it is their decision and there is nothing we can do about it.

I've withheld my car on three occasions.

One boy didn't take my advice and used his mother's car and had his test terminated half way through. When this happens, the examiner takes the car keys and walks back to the test centre leaving the candidate with the car. The keys are then presented to the person who brought the candidate for test, presumably with some suitable comment.

Another withdrawal was accepted as for the best and the test was passed at a second subsequent attempt.

The third withdrawal came about because Faye's brother thought she was ready for her test before I did. He persuaded her to book a test, she did as he asked but didn't tell me until it was two weeks away. This meant there was nothing in my book about it. When she did tell me, I found I had a test that afternoon and wouldn't be able to pick her up for her pre-test hour. To avoid this happening in the normal course of events, we quote a driving school code number on application forms thus avoiding double bookings.

This problem resulted in Faye cancelling lessons she had already booked, saying she was going to practice in a Fiat her dad had bought her. I didn't hear from her for about two months but shortly after she stopped driving with me, I was passing her house and noticed the right hand gate post and a large chunk of the stone wall in a sorry heap.

When she did call it was to ask if she could resume lessons. During the first one, I learned that her test had been cancelled by her dad. The Fiat had been written off as she attempted to enter their drive a bit too quickly in order to get out of the way of a bus.

"What did your dad say?" I wanted to know.

"He didn't say anything to me — not for 5 weeks"

She did have the grace to say that she didn't blame him. He did ask her to stop and let the bus pass but in her words -"we'd had one of THOSE LESSONS"

$$\cdot \cdot \textbf{L} \cdot \cdot$$

In the past, examiners had their own ways of signalling for an emergency stop to be performed. Consequently a variety of different signals were used. The examiner would demonstrate his method during his briefing to the candidate while they were parked up.

The method favoured by the examiner who tested my eldest son was the familiar one of tapping on the dashboard and calling stop. He briefed Alan at the top of a fairly steep downward gradient. After the briefing Alan drove on, the signal came and according to my son he performed a perfect emergency stop but the examiner's papers shot off his knee into the well down by the dual control pedals.

The examiner told Alan not to worry, it wasn't his fault and he was to drive on. He watched Alan make the necessary observations and move away. After asking him to take the road on the left at the bottom of the hill, he bent to retrieve his paperwork. Before he could straighten up again, a dog shot across the road in front of the car and Alan made his second emergency stop. The seat belt prevented the examiner banging his head but it didn't stop him saying, "bloody hell, what's going on?"

As a matter of interest, there is now a standard signal for emergency stops during the driving test — scheduled ones, that is.

Many young people start their driving lessons on their 17th Birthday. Providing this doesn't coincide with important exams, it's a very good idea. The power of concentration is there at that age and what better birthday prezzie could they get from Uncles and Aunts and of course mum and dad. Driving is for life whereas a box of chocolates is for half an hour.

It probably costs the average person between 300 and £500 to learn to drive. That may sound a lot of money but set it against the cost of a holiday and it becomes a sound investment. Leaving it a few years isn't going to make it any easier and it will, in all probability cost more to do so.

The only awkward factor with learning at 17 could be going away to University shortly after passing a test and not being able to drive for a few years. This doesn't have to be a serious problem as there will always be a refresher course that can be taken when studies are finished. I've given many such courses and usually three or four lessons are sufficient to regain confidence.

It isn't only students who take refresher courses. Quite a few people pass a driving test and for a variety of reasons, don't drive for some time afterwards. The most common reason is they don't have a car available.

Many people take lessons even though they are aware they will not be able to have access to a car afterwards but they have an ambition to do this thing, even if it is only to prove to themselves they can do it. Many of the people taking driving lessons at any one time are ladies at home on their own, husband at work, kids at school, housework done, nothing on television so they put the time to use in a constructive fashion and join the millions of other would-be traffic jam builders.

I'll tell you later about a lady who used driving lessons as a therapy to help her over the death of her husband.

A pupil who did have access to a car after she passed her test, called me about 15 months after passing to ask for a refresher course. She hadn't driven since she got her licence despite the family car being freely available. She was in her 50's and needed, in her case, a course of 8 lessons before she felt confident.

Two years later she called again asking for another refresher course. A slight bump in their car while her husband had been driving had put her off after the last one. It took a while longer this time to build up her confidence and when she was about ready for going it alone, she made one last request. 'Would I sit with her, in their car while she drove to her sister's house in Sheffield?'. I booked two hours off in my book and we drove to her sister's, had a cuppa and returned to Leeds. This was the task she set herself, to make sure she kept driving regularly, every fortnight she would visit her sister. She called me again about 4 weeks later and her opening words made me wince but everything was alright now, "I've cracked it at last, trouble is Ernie keeps wanting his car back"

The lady had spent a small fortune on lessons before passing her test and quite a bit afterwards despite having a car available from day one. That first drive unaccompanied is quite a step, the longer it's left the harder it becomes.

○ ○ 🖂 ○ ○

Like most A.D.I.'s I teach my pupils to 'palm' the gear lever. That is to say when they are about to change gear, I'd insist that they place the palm of their hand on the SIDE of the lever. In order to get first or second gear the palm would face away from the pupil and for gears 3, 4 and 5 it would face towards them. By closing their fingers around the top of the lever, their hand can't slip off. A few people tend to resist closing their fingers round it and have to be shown until they do it properly. Why they can't or won't close their fingers is beyond me, it looks so incongruous to have the hand flat and fingers outstretched.

Sally was one such pupil. She palmed correctly but kept her fingers straight. Gradually she succumbed to my requests to 'close your fingers'

One of the first things you would notice about Sally, would be her finger nails. She was in her 20's, bright and had a good job. Her fingernails were always long, shaped and red, her appearance was important in her job and of course her nails were part of the overall effect she was creating. One day we were approaching a red traffic light that I felt would change to green just before we got to the line. I mentioned this to her and asked her to go from 4th gear to third in order that we might keep moving through the junction.

To make sure she got the message, I said, "go from 4 to 3, that's straight forward, palm facing *you* and you're the one wearing the yellow dress." She went 4 to 1 palm facing me, fingers STRAIGHT.

She even caught me with my clutch pedal not covered and the resultant engine braking, as she shot off the clutch, jerked her forward. Her hand slipped off the gear lever and hit the radio. Ping, ping, ping — three of her fingernails whizzed passed me and onto the back seat.

Sally had to make a serious contribution to my swear box and I was able to see why she wore false fingernails. We found two of them after the lesson but the other one didn't appear until a few weeks later when I was cleaning under the swab of the back seat.

Jimmy was a very large, pleasant 35 year old West Indian. He had two characteristics, an extremely loud voice and he liked his booze. Because of his voice he would go through life with no secrets. He could not talk quietly. Even when he whispered, he could be heard above the noise of my diesel engine in first gear.

Jimmy had lessons Tuesday and Friday evenings after he'd finished work as a foreman in a plastics factory. He lived alone in a terraced house from where he started and finished his lessons.

At the start of his sixth lesson he asked if he could just have 55 minutes instead of a full hour. Thinking he probably wanted to catch a T.V. programme, I said that was alright and I'd add the 5 minutes onto the end of his next lesson. He then said he wanted 55 minute lessons each time. I asked him why. In reporting his reply, I mean no insult to West Indian speak.

"We passes an Offy at de end of mah street on de way home. Ah wants you to wait for me while ah loads up wid mah cans"

So we did this twice a week, whether his lesson lasted 55 or 60 minutes, we'd stop at the Offy. He'd come out with a carrier bag full of 4 packs.

On one occasion I wanted something for home so I joined him, while I looked round the store for the Bitter Lemon, I heard Jimmy announcing to everyone "That's John, mah driving instructor"

Of course some wag said the obvious. "Is he driving you to drink then Jimmy?"

Jimmy liked that and from then on, as each lesson neared it's end, my ears were bombarded by, "come on, it's time you drove me to drink"

Apart from the G.B.H. of the eardrums, we got on very well and as his test approached he asked me if I would sit-in with him.

If a candidate wants someone to sit-in with them on test, it is up to them to make the request to the examiner. Providing it is within reason, the request will be granted. They would turn it down, I suppose, if someone wanted their rugby team in with them.

Jimmy's request for my presence in the back of the car on his test, was made thus in his loud, loud voice to a full waiting room, "Dis fella's driven me to drink for de last tree months, ah might as well have him on mah test, is dat alright wid you Boss?"

It was, he passed and I've got for sale — one pair of used ear plugs.

In Leeds we have a very active Driving Instructors' Association. One of its attractions is a Golf Society. When it was first formed, the organiser, I'll call him Bryan, because that is his name, was a man short. Somewhere in the dim distant past, I had slipped up and mentioned that, once upon a time, I had swung a club or two. This rash statement saw me 'volunteered' to make the numbers up for the first competition.

I was really looking forward to the agonies I'd suffer the following day. It was over 10 years since I had last dug up a golf course!

The day before the competition it poured with rain, we had an overnight frost and it was still below zero when we turned up at the course, all bright eyed and bushy tailed, all that is except one of us. Imagine if you will, it was to be my first game of golf in over 10 years, the course was rock hard with pools scattered here and there covered in ice. It was a freezing February day on a course splendidly situated around and on top of the highest hills in the whole of the Leeds area. (You owe me Bryan!)

To cap everything, I'd gone into the loft to get my clubs down the evening before and I realised only then, that I had sold them about 5 years previously. Not wanting to let them down, well actually wanting *desperately* to let them down but not daring, I played in ordinary shoes, in a totally inadequate anorak and with my daughter's half set of clubs.

They didn't invite me back, I think that's because I won the raffle afterwards. It took a couple of days to thaw out and a week to get my back in line with the rest of me.

There is a great deal of camaraderie between driving instructors in the Leeds area. This often surprises Guest Speakers we have at our Association meetings. This spirit is helped by the Association itself, we have over 70 members and we pull together in a remarkable fashion when you consider we are in competition with each other for work.

A.D.I.'s who are ill know they can depend on finding someone available to help out with lessons and especially with tests.

One member was very fortunate in this respect. He suffered a mild heart attack and during the six or so weeks he was going to be off work he had six tests booked. Without any covering help this could have been very unfortunate for his pupils. All his tests were covered and indeed, most of his lessons were sorted out as well, which meant he still had a business to go back to after his illness.

Part of an examiner's brief when taking a test is to inspect the vehicle's tyres for roadworthiness. If he considers any of them to be unsafe, or illegal, he has the power to abort the test.

Going into the test centre on one occasion, I noticed the rear off-side tyre of another driving school car was quite flat. Usually I like to get into the waiting room just as the examiner is coming out of the office, this saves pupils chewing their fingernails. On this occasion my pupil wanted to have a cigarette before her test, so we arrived at the centre earlier than normal. This early arrival meant I had time to dash into the waiting room and alert the instructor to his problem.

Fortunately there is a filling station almost next door to the test centre, so he was able to get some air in his tyre and get the car back in place before examiner and candidate got to it. He couldn't explain what he had been doing because if the examiner suspected the tyre might be faulty and deflate during the test, he may have aborted it. The A.D.I. sat with everything crossed until they got back - still inflated.

°°🛇°°

The following story is not about driving instruction but it does involve an A.D.I. Cliff has now retired and he cheerfully delved into his experiences for me. As well as being an A.D.I. he was also a qualified P.S.V. (Public Service Vehicle) driver and as such he drove coaches for a well known Leeds holiday company.

One Saturday he was contracted to drive a party from a Working Mens' Club to Blackpool for a day trip. On arrival in Blackpool, he made sure his passengers knew both the name of the coach-park and the departure time before they all made their way into town.

To Cliff's enormous surprise everyone was back on time, Cliff started up the coach and moved towards the coach-park exit. As he approached it he saw a body lying across the road blocking the exit. He stopped and asked the two men in the front seat next to him to go and sort the body out. The two men got out and spent 3 or 4 minutes over the body.

Impatience on the coach was growing, when one of the men came back and said to Cliff, "He's absolutely stoned but he lives in Leeds and he has missed his bus back, can we take him?"

"No," said Cliff. "It's against company rules, if they don't come with us, they can't go back with us."

"Nay lad, we can't leave him there in that state," said the carer.

Passenger power prevailed and Cliff had to let them bring the body on board. It was put in a spare seat by a window and slept there the whole way to Leeds, even when the men got out to water the daisies and stock up again at a halfway house.

Arriving back at the Working Mens' Club, the passengers started getting off the coach, this worried Cliff, because no-one was paying any attention to the body. As the last couple were leaving, Cliff stopped counting his tip and queried with them, what they intended doing about it.

"Nay lad, tha brought 'im, tha see to 'im"

So Cliff was lumbered, the body was still asleep and still in the position it had been put when it was brought aboard in Blackpool. He plainly couldn't take the bus back to the garage with a body on board.

Cliff managed to rouse the body sufficiently to discover where it lived when it wasn't comatose. Middleton is a suburb of

Leeds in the opposite direction to the one Cliff would dearly like to be driving in. However he decided he had no option if he wanted to keep his job, so, Middleton it was. He knew his way around and found the body's address. By this time the body was out of it again and making more noise than the bus was.

It was now 2.30 in the morning, the house was in darkness. Cliff knocked on the door a few times and eventually a light came on upstairs and a bedroom window opened.

"Who's there?" hollered a voice.

"Does Terry Andrews live here?"

"Yes but he's not here, he's in Morecambe on his holidays"

"No he's not, he's on my coach I've just brought him from Blackpool"

"He can't be, he's gone to Morecambe for a week and he only went this morning"

"Look I'm telling you, he's on my coach, now come down here and help me get him inside the house or I'll dump him in the road. I've to get this coach back in the garage and get home, I'm working in the morning"

She came down and Cliff got rid of Terry and returned his coach.

It appears, the coach driver who took Terry and his mates to Morecambe was staying over night to bring a party back the next morning and he'd volunteered to take some of them into Blackpool for the evening and it was *that* coach Terry had missed.

For his good deed, Cliff was reprimanded by the company on two counts. He shouldn't have abused company rules by bringing a non-fare paying passenger back and would you believe, the body complained about being brought back to Leeds against his wishes.

Now I guess there will be a lot of people who would complain about being taken to Leeds against their wishes but that really was a liberty.

For many years I have driven and taught in Renault cars. I know this will be tempting fate but I have always been delighted with them. Mechanically and bodywise I find they are tough and reliable and in my line of business they come in for some rugged treatment. The seating position is good for learners, in that a good field of vision is available to front and rear. In some makes of car, diminutive pupils have to nearly stand up to see a kerb out of the back window.

The main quibble I have with modern car design is not restricted to Renaults. In the interests of streamlining, some years ago, designers removed the rain water gully from the roof of the car. This gully used to channel all the rain from the roof of the car down the sides of the front and rear windscreens. This rainwater now just sits there, on the roof, until the car is driven round a corner or bend and it then whooshes down the side of the car unless the front window is open. Then it has the unpleasant habit of depositing itself down whichever side of the body is nearest the open window. The nature of our job requires that we do a lot of talking and if we don't have the windows down, there is a tendency for them to mist up on wet days.

As it's the pupil who is paying, it is only decent that it should be our window that is open, consequently the left side of our body develops rheumatics before the remainder, caused by the soakings we get. Bring back the gully !!

Permit me another little moan at car designers.

Why don't more of you specify 'Bolt through wheel trims?' The funny thing about wheel trims is how often you see them lying at the side of the road where they lie after spinning off a car like a flying saucer. Until that is, you lose one of your own. Then they all vanish and become as rare as hen's teeth. If you do find one, after days of searching, it's either too big or it's squashed. If they're bolted on with the wheel it will be safer as well as cheaper.

·· 🚗 ··

Phil told me of the time he was waiting for a pupil outside Leeds University. He'd got there early and had parked up just off the main road in a lay-by. He was reading his Highway Code because he's one who likes to keep up to date. He looked up and spied a familiar figure coming towards him. It was a lady, he knew her face but couldn't give her a name. Like me, Phil uses a headboard to advertise his school.

The lady got nearer and still Phil couldn't think where he knew her from. She was loaded with carrier bags and her glasses were swinging round her neck on a chain. She saw Phil's car and headed for it at a gallop,

"This is going to be embarrassing, I can't think of her name and she looks a bit posh to call love"

As she came alongside, Phil wound his window down desperately thinking what to say when she acknowledged him. She reached his window and gasped breathlessly,
"Thank God for that, I thought you'd be gone before I got here. You are free aren't you?"

The very clear voice and the roundness of the tones made Phil realise instantly where he knew the lady from. She was a star in a very popular and funny T.V. programme and she had mistaken Phil's car - with his headboard - for a taxi.

Phil was a bit disappointed to have to say, "Sorry Miss Jones, I'm not a taxi"

His Leonard Rossiter impression didn't make up for her disappointment and I don't think that what she said, as she realised her mistake, was quite in character for Miss Jones!

I had a strange experience when a new pupil told me, on his first lesson, that he had already driven my car. He could drive, in a manner of speaking, but my car was new when I'd picked it up a couple of months earlier so how could he have driven it before? He kept me guessing throughout the lesson during which he displayed a rather crude self taught ability to 'move' the car as opposed to driving it.

He worked for a company that valet cars prior to them being collected by their new owners. He'd been responsible for preparing mine and he'd even put the new roof sign on. Because he could 'drive' his company assumed he was licensed to do so. Having spruced up a car he would then have to drive it to the collection point to await its owner.

When I saw him drive on his first lesson, I was disturbed to think he'd already been responsible for driving my new pride and joy through some quite busy corners and junctions. I won't mention any names but I do know his company now ask to see employees' driving licences.

If a bus lane has no times displayed on the signs announcing it to be a bus and cycle lane, then it is a 24 hour one and should not be used by vehicles other than buses or bikes. If the signs display times, e.g. 7.30 a.m. - 9.30 a.m. Mon.-Fri. then outside those hours it is a normal part of the highway and should be used by any vehicle.

One Sunday morning a pupil was driving us along a bus lane marked as above. A taxi, coming out of a junction in front and to our left, stopped with half the vehicle effectively blocking our path about 20 metres away. There was a continuous stream of traffic coming along in the right hand lane, as we couldn't pull out and go round the taxi so we had to stop.

I was only a few metres away from the driver and my window was down. Leaning out of it I was about to ask him to pull back (and give him a mucky look) when he called out, "Why are you in the bus lane?"

I pointed to the sign to his left. He bent down and looked back at it. Having absorbed the information displayed thereon, he turned to me and said, "It's Sunday, what sort of driving instructor are you, you don't even know what day it is".

The worrying thing is, because of his occupation, I suppose he would class himself as a professional driver.

No matter who we are or what we do and how well we do it, we all like to have the old ego massaged at times.

I really thought my turn had come in an opening conversation on 17 year old Rachel's first lesson. Normally when we pick up a pupil for their first lesson, we'd drive them to a reasonably quiet spot in order to go through the 'controls' lesson undisturbed.

This drive gives us the chance to get to know a bit about the pupil and attempt to put them at ease. It's always interesting to know how the pupil came to contact my school so I asked Rachel who had recommended me. She told me that she had asked around at school among her friends who were having lessons or had recently had them.

Hello I thought, I like the way this is going and I could feel my chest starting to swell out a bit.

"I'm taking my exams soon" she went on, "but I wanted to start driving as well. Because of my exams, I can't afford to get involved with anybody until they're finished, so I came to you 'cos you're much older than most of my friends instructors." I never did get on well with that girl.

Some people, having failed a driving test, feel that a change of instructor is called for. In some cases it may be the right thing to do but if you get on well, stay together and have another attempt as a team. If you feel your A.D.I. is wasting your time, then by all means try elsewhere.

In common with most instructors I've had people ring me up suggesting they feel they are getting nowhere. They've had 30 lessons and still their A.D.I. hasn't mentioned applying for a test. I'm not saying that all A.D.I.'s are saints but after an assessment drive, it's often the case that the pupil isn't a natural driver and even after all those lessons they are nowhere near test standard. I gave an example earlier where I felt a lady was being held back for unfair reasons but it's usually the case that the pupil is simply not good enough to test.

It has to be said that for some people, 30 lessons can be nowhere near enough and yet many, many more will pass in less than 20, it depends on a person's aptitude for driving.

It is always pleasing to see pupils pass their test, especially the ones to whom driving didn't come naturally. They were the ones who were, to say the least, frustrating at first. The ones who must have got fed up hearing their instructor say....

"No, *gently* up on the clutch pedal —

Never mind — handbrake on — into neutral.

Let's start again — switch on — clutch down — into 1st gear —

— hold your handbrake — Ooooops, no we were not ready for the clutch yet.

Handbrake on — into neutral — switch on — clutch down —

10 minutes later — Never mind — handbrake on — neutral — switch on".

I admit I've often thought about referring some pupils to friends who teach automatic driving. I've always been a one-car school, teaching manual gear changing but many schools provide both options. It surprises me that more people, when learning to drive, don't choose the automatic option.

"Don't you worry Mr Jones just take your time"

It is much easier to pick up and the price differential between automatic and manual cars has narrowed over the years. The drawback is that if you pass your test in an automatic vehicle, you are restricted to that type and would have to take another test should you wish to go manual.

There is quite a different technique required if you switch from manual to automatic, which you can legally do and it is something which should not be attempted without some form of instruction.

Providing ALL candidates turn up, the D.S.A.'s schedule allows it's examiners to conduct 8 tests per day from it's network of driving test centres. At some centres, tests can be had during evenings or on a Saturday morning at a premium charge. In areas where there is a limited population, test centres may be open at certain hours only.

The first test starts at 8.40 a.m. It is usual for an instructor to pick their pupil up an hour before the test is due to start. This hour, although pupils look upon it as a lesson, should really be for a bit of general driving practice and to run through the manoeuvres once or twice. It gives them confidence to think about that hour in the days running up to their test but tuition should be complete by then.

The 8.40 test requires A.D.I.'s to be picking their pupil up at about 7.30 a.m. That's a ghastly hour for people like us, cosseted by driving around in warm cars all day, especially on a cold January morning, hoping nay, praying the car will start.

I'm a keen gardener, not good just keen. My definition of a keen gardener is one who can squash a slug between the fingers without going "Aaaaargh" Little ones up to an inch long, thumb and forefinger, quick squeeze and flick 'em back on the garden where hopefully, all they've taken out goes back in. The big ones are more difficult, if you squeeze a 4" slug it just bulges out at both ends, so they need dispatching between the heel of your boot and a hard place.

I was due to pick a pupil up for his 8.40 test. For some reason I hadn't set the alarm correctly, consequently I was coming out of the house 10 minutes later than I should have been doing.

Monday morning, clean grey trousers, briefcase in hand, sprinting down the drive to the garage. I spied a 4" slug making it's way across to my newly planted marigolds, I could almost see it licking it's lips in anticipation. I broke stride to squash the demon with my right heel but my aim was a bit off. I hit the slug at one end and as my left leg came through it was just in time to catch the entire contents of the slug's insides.

It is amazing how much nature can cram into one 4" slug. It seemed as though half a ton of it was clinging to the inside of my left trouser leg. At that stage I'd only time to kick the bulk of it off and I spent most of a toilet roll and Tom's test getting as much of it off as I could in the test centre loo.

Chapter Six
HIGH TECH AND OLD TIMES

If we question pupils about what we are doing and why we are doing it, it makes them think about the situation and not simply accept it. It also helps the instructor determine how much of his teaching is being taken in. Some pupils, quite understandably, find it difficult to drive and talk at the same time, particularly while they are at an early stage.

One such pupil was a very shy boy, yes they still exist, he would answer my questions but never spoke an unsolicited word. I changed my car after he'd had 7 or 8 lessons and it had an infra-red locking system.

His parents lived in a house with a long winding drive which Simon wasn't up to managing yet, so I left the car as usual, outside the drive when I went to pick him up. As we came out of the gate and approached the car, I operated the central locking device and unlocked the car from a distance with a substantial click.

"Hey that's terrific, how did you do that?" he asked.

His first question after all this time and all I could do was to say lamely, "I pressed the dimple on this key"

At last he wanted to know something and I couldn't explain how a beam transmitted from a key 5 metres away, could unlock 5 doors on the vehicle. I'm an absolute dummy where electronics are concerned. Pocket calculators are still high tech to me, in fact, I need the R.A.C. when the battery goes on my torch. However my new car and it's gadget got Simon talking and it wasn't quite so hard after that. He tried to get me interested in computers but I'm afraid he was on a hiding to nothing and I still don't think I'd know a floppy disk from a table mat. I'd certainly find the latter of more use.

Simon's reluctance to talk at first caused a bit of a problem but so can the other side of the coin.

Jean was a middle aged lady who, over a period of 8 years had failed 12 tests. She had even been on a television programme about people who had failed many driving tests.
I was her sixth instructor and she never stopped talking. Home was a small semi-detached house she shared with her husband, son, daughter, daughter's husband and daughter's daughter and she never stopped talking. She did part time nursing, part-time office work, part-time dance instruction, Brownies and she looked after her very sick parents who lived a short distance away. A very nice person but she NEVER stopped talking. I think she came nearer to driving me round the bend than anyone before or since. I learned all the above in her first lesson. Did I say she never - yes I must have.

The first test she had with me she failed, that was number 13, I pleaded with the examiner afterwards but he wouldn't change his mind.

Not for the first time the big stick had to come out. We'd had serious words before but this time they were really serious. I'd tried before to enlist the help of her husband but it was no use, he'd been trying to get her to stop for breath for nearly 20 years.

So every time she said anything that wasn't relative to what we were doing, I stopped the car. We didn't travel very far for a couple of lessons but it started to work and marvellously she passed her test at the next attempt.

As I walked to my car, I passed the examiner in the street and he said,
"By heck, she can talk"

..🕮..

Planning a working week is important. A sensible cost-conscious A.D.I. will attempt to keep his 'dead time' down to a minimum. If he has a number of pupils at the far side of this patch, he will try and get them to have lessons on the same day. It makes sense to cut down as far as possible on wasted fuel as well as on wear and tear on both vehicle and driver.

Cutting down on waste reminds me of the time before I became an A.D.I.

I had just started to work for a large national food company. The Managing Director asked me to familiarise myself with the Company's personnel and working methods by travelling around some of it's 43 branches for my first six weeks.

Half way through this period I met up with the M.D when, by coincidence, he was visiting the same branch as me. He asked me how I was getting on and what my thoughts were up to now. Although I was very much the new boy he was very serious. I told him I was worried by the amount of stock that was being wasted by careless handling in all the branches I'd visited so far. He showed a great deal of concern and over a cuppa we discussed the subject. He didn't have much time so he suggested I cut short my tour and meet with him in his office the next week. We made a date in our diaries for my visit and as he put his diary back in his pocket he took out a thin booklet. He signed one of the sheets, tore it out and gave it to me. I looked at it and couldn't believe it.

Three weeks earlier, this company had let me have an expensive company car. The M.D of the company had just handed me a rail warrant to travel FIRST CLASS to London to report to him on WASTE in the company.

Was his face red when he saw that detailed in my report the following week! No, he didn't sack me, his sense of humour probably stopped him. I also found out that day that they spared no expense on their boardroom lunches either.

A friend of mine finished his lessons about 7.30 one evening and was heading home round the Leeds ring road on a stretch of dual carriageway governed by the national speed limit. He'd been followed by a Panda car for a few miles. Just before a gap in the central reservation, the police driver moved in front of Andy and directed him to pull over.

Both cars having stopped the P.C. got out and walked back to Andy, the conversation went like this:-
"Are you a driving instructor?"
"Yes"
"Are you aware you've been breaking the speed limit for the last 3.½ miles?"
"No"
"Well you have. I've clocked you doing 68 mph for virtually all that distance"

"Are you going to book me?"
"You should be setting an example to other drivers and keep within the speed limit"
"I agree with you, are you going to book me?"
"I ought to"
"I'll tell you what, let's turn round through that gap just up there and we'll go to your station, it's about 3.½ miles back up the road, where you came on my tail and you can book me in comfort"
"Why are you so keen on being booked?" I was going to let you go with a warning"
"I just want to see your desk sergeant's face when you tell him you're booking me for doing 68 on a 70 mph road"

The P.C. was not convinced until Andy produced a copy of the Highway Code.

He's got a sadistic streak that one.

Being on fairly busy roads most of the week we see many acts of dodgy driving. Following too close behind, cutting in front and pulling out at junctions when it would have been safer to have waited and that's just other instructors and police drivers, the rest of the general public are almost as bad.

I'd just been briefing a pupil about coping with roundabouts. As you'd imagine, it's an important part of a learner's early stage development. Because traffic 'only' comes from the right as you join a roundabout, pupils sometimes find it hard to see why they must always look left as well, before emerging. This was a "Pure Gold' lesson. Sharon didn't take my instruction to look left, she started onto the roundabout but I 'dualled' her.

Coming from her left, the wrong way round the roundabout, was an old Morris Minor driven by a very small, elderly gentleman who appeared to have great difficulty seeing over the wheel. We saw him off the roundabout and Sharon didn't make the same mistake again.

The worst bit of driving I've ever seen was perpetrated by a bus driver in rush hour traffic. I was 'with pupil' approaching a very busy junction controlled by traffic lights. We were about 30 metres from the lights when they changed to red. No problem, a quick mirror check showed a bus about the same 30 metres behind with nothing in between. Gentle breaking brought us to the line. Suddenly I was aware of the bus picking up speed and hurtling past us and on through the lights which, by now had been red for quite some time.
The bus was packed, it could have been a disaster.

Something very fortuitous saved a calamity that evening.

At that particular junction, traffic only came from our right. By the time the bus went through, the traffic queue on the right would have had a green light showing for a few seconds already. First in line in that queue was another driving school car and he had been very slow getting moving. I'm sure his inability to get off the mark prevented the bus smashing into him. The A.D.I. in the car realised what had happened and he wiped his brow as he passed in front of us.

The habit nowadays, particularly in rush hours, seems to be to start moving forward on red and amber instead of waiting for green. It is a sobering thought that had it been an experienced driver first in line when that light changed, it could have been carnage.
Just what was in the bus driver's mind, I can't think. He was at least 50 metres away from those lights when they went red.

Eddie had a pupil out on a lesson, she'd had about 15 already and was quite capable. She was driving along a straight, quiet stretch of road when she moved out to the middle and came back in again. Eddie woke up at this point but said nothing until she did it again a short time later for all the world as though she was passing a parked vehicle. As she came in the second time Eddie asked her what she was doing.

"Passing that parked car" she replied.

Is she having me on? thought Eddie.

Then she started to move out again for no reason.

"Pull in on the left Karen" Eddie instructed. "What's going on?"

"I'm passing parked cars" Karen insisted looking at Eddie.
As she did so Eddie saw her eyes and she was 'out of it', as the saying goes.

"The fire was lit but no smoke was going up the chimney" Eddie told me. He knew her boyfriend was into drugs but it hadn't been a problem with Karen as long as he'd known her. So, a quick shuffle about with the seating arrangements and Eddie returned Karen from whence she came ASAP. It could have been very nasty for Eddie, he made enquiries and it appears that had they been stopped while Karen was driving, Eddie could have been charged with aiding and abetting.

I think the following must be a fairly common feeling among women test candidates. Whenever I've mentioned it to other A.D.I.'s they've come across a similar reaction.

I was taking a 30 year old lady for her first test. We'd parked outside the centre, locked the car and started our walk to the waiting room when she said to me, "I feel absolutely dreadful, look at me I'm shivering and I've got butterflies like wood pigeons in my stomach. I think I'd rather have a baby than take this wretched test"

The standard answer is, "You've left it a bit late, half an hour earlier and we could have adjusted the seats" It really was too late for that now, the examiners were coming out of their office, so I told her to see how the examiner felt about it.
She passed, so I don't know what went on.

Among the able bodied, the hardest group of people to teach are the ones with no control initially over their left leg. Those of you who found driving even remotely easy to pick up, spare a thought for those fellow beings who suffer from whiplash left leg syndrome.

I've referred already to the lady who passed her test in order to leave her husband, she came into this category. Another one, again a lady, slightly older this time but no marital problems I was aware of, had the same affliction. We'd be ready to set off and BANG, she was off that clutch pedal as though it was red hot.

For non-drivers, the clutch pedal coming up smoothly and steadily connects the power of the engine to the wheels and enables the vehicle to move away. If the pedal is allowed to come up too quickly, the engine cuts out or 'stalls' as it is more commonly called.

Instructors are not supposed to touch pupils, otherwise it would be simple to put a hand on the pupil's knee and allow the leg and foot to come up slowly but we can't do this. We'd never try it with a female pupil and if a male pupil suggested we do it — we still wouldn't do it, but that's another story!!

We have a dual control clutch pedal we can use as a last resort to get some movement out of a lesson other than jerks and kangaroo bounces. The first time I used my dual control on this lady's lesson she thought she'd mastered it, I had to go and spoil it then and tell her differently. She soon realised when it went BANG next time that she still had a bit of work to do.

"That's what I call style."

Eventually some semblance of control appeared and steadily it got better. This lady was a fork lift truck instructor and although she gave me a hard time in the beginning, once she got things moving and we got around to the manoeuvres, I found she was mustard when it came to reversing. I must have bored her silly telling her she could drive backwards better than forwards.

Before Cliff, the coach driver, retired he had been an A.D.I. for many years and a few of the stories I'm recounting come from him.

He told me the following one which goes back to the days when examiners expected hand signals to be demonstrated during a test. Today it is sufficient for candidates to know them in case they should be needed.

During the journey to the test centre, the instructor pressed upon his pupil the importance of giving his hand signals effectively, "When you give your slowing down or left turn signal, really get into it." For anyone not sure, both these signals should be given with the right arm fully extended out of the window with the palm facing down. For the slowing down signal, the hand is lowered and raised 3 or 4 times slowly and the arm is then withdrawn and the hand replaced on the steering wheel. To turn left the hand is used to describe 3 or 4 forward circles slowly and then withdrawn.

This particular instructor definitely had his own way with hand signals.

"I've really got the hang of the hand signals now."

He'd tell his pupils to, "Really get into it and disturb the gravel on the road with those fingertips"

Although it's a bit over the top, I think that is a marvellous turn of phrase.

So, suitably under orders, the lad set off on his test. The A.D.I. was waiting outside the test centre when his car came back. He was surprised to see the examiner get out as soon as the car stopped. He wondered why he wasn't asking his pupil his Highway Code questions.

The examiner called him over and said in a quiet voice,
"He's a bit upset, he was hand signalling to turn left and an Alsatian rushed up and grabbed his arm. His hand and arm are cut a bit and he's lost the sleeve off his jumper"

It gives a whole new meaning to 'get right' into those hand signals!

*****

I've never had to teach anyone who didn't have some command of English. In fact a group of Nigerians I've had all spoke better English than wot I do.

Non-English speakers will require an interpreter with them on lessons if their instructor doesn't speak their language. This will also apply to their test as well. It seems in Leeds that if an A.D.I. satisfies one Chinese person with his instruction he will have a never ending supply of Chinese knocking on his door for lessons.

A couple of students from Namibia gave me a few problems in this direction but my difficulties were small compared to theirs. Not only did they have my Yorkshire accent to interpret but they had the English infra-structure to contend with. They were studying at Leeds University and until they arrived in England they had never seen roundabouts or traffic lights.

You can imagine the problems they had coming to terms with our road and traffic conditions.

I've seen some recent film of Windhoek, the Namibian capital city and it appears as though it has been modernised now. The two students have gone back to Namibia now so it will be fairly easy for them after learning to drive amid the throng in Leeds. The boy student told me if he didn't get the job he hoped for, he felt he'd be able to make a comfortable living teaching people to drive.

Teaching through an interpreter is going to be fraught with problems especially if the interpreter can't drive. One of the problems is going to be terminology. Although we teach the same thing, A.D.I.'s are all individuals and have their own way of explaining how to perform certain functions. Coming to a roundabout for instance, after a few years doing the same thing it's a bit like switching to automatic pilot. The instructions come forth as though they were pre-programmed. Using an interpreter will make it necessary to re-think these instructions and how they are to be passed on. They must of course be given in time for the interpreter to do his translating.

One of my instinctive phrases used to be 'Tell people where you're going' as we approached a junction if a signal was required and the pupil was at the stage where they should be doing their own thinking.

On one occasion when I was teaching a middle-aged comedian, I wanted him to take the second turning on the left. He had plenty of time as there would be about 100 metres between the first and second turnings. Between the two there was a bus stop on the right hand side of the road with half a dozen people waiting at it. He left his signal late so I reminded him in my customary way. Through his half open window he called to the bus queue,
"I'm going left just down the road, anyone want to come?"

Never again.

'Tell people where you're going' has become, 'Have you forgotten your signal?'

··🚗··

The following was detailed to me by the instructor, who was waiting immediately behind the car in question.

A driving school car, with a young lady at the wheel, was waiting for the green light at a busy junction. A small queue of cars was forming behind.

Red and amber came on and she prepared to go. As the green came on, she must have succumbed to pressure from behind. She came off the clutch pedal too quickly and the car stalled. She was seen to make it safe and start the engine again but sod's law had it's evil way and she stalled again (Sod's law says, if you are going to stall it once, you'll do it twice)

By now the light was red and as the road was narrow, no-one had gone through. The instructor could be seen telling her what to do — hold on, it's changing again but it wasn't her day and she stalled once more. This was too much for one of the 'expert' drivers behind and he sounded his horn viciously. He probably hadn't noticed a police car had now joined the queue, which by now was stretching quite a way round a long right hand bend.

A loud hailer on the police car burst into life with the instruction,

"Will the driver who is sounding his horn please refrain from doing so, the young lady is doing her best and that arrogant attitude won't help her"

The red light had returned by now and still no-one had moved through the junction.

Instructions were again being fed to the pupil by her A.D.I.. Red and amber, she got ready, in first gear, clutch pedal at the biting point, hand on handbrake — GREEN — clutch pedal up, handbrake off — wrong order, stalled again!!

No vicious sounding horn this time, just a voice coming over the loud hailer, which plainly should have been switched off,

"Christ, the silly bitch has done it again"

Time I think, for the AD.I.'s dual controls to start earning their keep.

..🆔..

Apart from a push-bike, my first form of transport was an immensely <u>un</u>reliable but VERY big and powerful Calthorpe motor bike. It had a hand gear change on the side of the petrol tank and I'd drive it away from home many a time and <u>push</u> it back. I bought it for £15 from a 'friend' and sold it for £5 to a scrap dealer three months later. It would be worth a small fortune now. The only benefit I derived from it was to be a pair of more muscular legs to go with the bad back it gave me.

Next came a reliable 125cc BSA Bantam bike which took my wife-to-be and me all over, much to the consternation of our parents. Neither set of parents had ever felt the need to pollute the atmosphere with fossil fuel fumes. After the Bantam came a 650cc Matchless Twin exhaust job. That was a beautiful machine. After the popping of the Bantam, the twin cylinders of the Matchless were music to the ears and the acceleration was out of this world, literally almost, on a few occasions.

Married life brought a baby and sidecar. My wife didn't mind having the baby but she drew the line at the sidecar so we had to buy that! It seemed criminal lumbering my magnificent Matchless with a sidecar but it had to be — my wife would not stay at home and I wanted to eat.

Two wheels eventually gave way to four in the shape of an Austin A35 van.

We were now running a business and stock had to be carried back and forth.

Cometh the van, cometh the common cold. While I was riding bikes I never suffered with a cold. Strangely though, once I was using covered transport, I started with colds and was never without one for the first three months.

Driving tuition in the van was provided by a friendly garage owner who also let me keep the van in his workshop out of harm's way when I wasn't using it. After I'd had 4 or 5 outings with him, a friend of my father, one Nobby Clarke, offered to give me some driving experience one Sunday afternoon.

Nobby came by bus from the other side of Leeds and after familiarising himself with the van, we were ready to set off. I got the impression Nobby didn't do much driving himself, he was very reluctant to let me take the handbrake off and make a start. He made me demonstrate using the footbrake time and time again. I found myself wondering what sort of hold my father had over him to let him put himself in such a position.

After we did set off he didn't instil much confidence in me by pointing out approaching vehicles and he would have me drive almost in the middle of the road, 'in case anyone comes out from the left.' Nobby didn't have a great deal of confidence in me and that feeling was reciprocated.

After about 1.½ hours he seemed to be getting more and more agitated, I thought I was doing quite well. I suppose he was working on the law of averages, we'd not had an accident in the first hour so we were due one in the second. He wasn't telling me where to go, just chipping in with the odd word of 'advice' every so often, so it was pure coincidence we passed the end of the street where he lived. He told me this and without thinking,

I suggested dropping him off to save him having to get the bus back. It wasn't bravado, simply that neither of us gave a thought to the situation. So when he said O.K., I did.

The realisation of what we had done hit me about 10 minutes later when I was climbing a steep hill with a set of traffic lights half way up. I was a long way from them when they went to green. I can remember thinking 'Stay green, stay green"
They did, I coped and got home in one piece. I often used that hill on lessons and I could still hear myself saying 'stay green'.

When I got home, my wife asked,"Where's Nobby, is he staying for tea?"
She couldn't believe he'd bailed out on the other side of Leeds.

About half an hour later we had a nervous sounding Nobby on the phone. He was most apologetic. He was out of the car and I'd gone before he realised what we'd done. I couldn't resist telling him about the dented wing and how the police would be in touch with him by morning.

This happened in the early part of 1956. Later that year, the governments of Britain and France were to fall out with Egypt over the Suez Canal. This resulted in the Egyptians blockading the Canal by sinking ships in the shipping lanes. This meant that oil tankers bound for Britain and Europe from the Persian Gulf had to sail around the African continent, taking much longer of course and incurring greater transport costs. This caused an oil shortage which was to last well into 1957. The result, of what rapidly became a crisis, was petrol rationing. Petrol could only be bought on production of coupons. We saw something else happen then, which wouldn't be allowed to happen today. In retrospect it didn't have a great deal of rationale even then. Learner drivers were allowed to drive unaccompanied. Exactly how that helped the petrol situation I have no idea.

On a personal level, this meant I could practice as much as I wanted in my van, without waiting for friends to sit with me. Fortunately everyone seemed to take things steadily and I cannot recall a sudden surge in the accident figures. Of course there wouldn't have been a quarter of today's traffic about then.

So, for a driving test, you could turn up on your own, take your test and - pass or fail - you would drive away on your own.

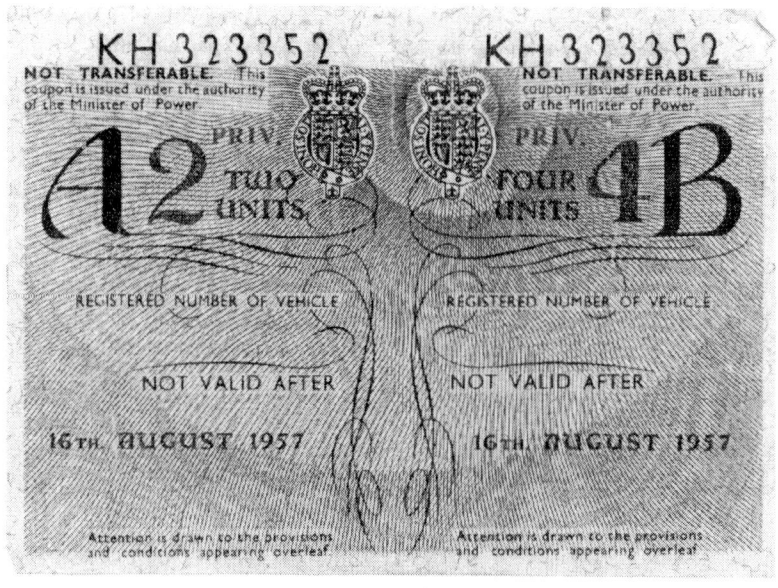

1957 Petrol Coupons 2 Gallons and 4 Gallons

Rather like the elderly chap I saw once.

My pupil was about to go into the test centre, when a car with a single occupant pulled up behind us. The driver got out and cool as you like, fitted 'L'plates to front and back of his car. He then walked in front of us into the centre. He'd obviously been before because he took all the correct turns, pushed the doors that had to be pushed and pulled the one which usually catches newcomers out. He sat and waited for the examiner and took his test.

I saw him come back but I don't think he passed as he waited for the examiner to move away before getting out and removing his 'L'plates. I did mention it in passing to the examiner at a later date but his reply was, "Nothing to do with me, I just test 'em".

The following two stories come from Cliff and both occurred at the time of the oil crisis.

A man arrived at the test centre legally unaccompanied and left his car in the car park. When the examiner called him the necessary documentation was completed and he correctly read a number plate. They got in the car outside the test centre and the candidate was asked to drive on and follow the road ahead until asked to do otherwise. After about a mile or so the candidate was obviously not having a happy time with his gears. The examiner asked him to park up on the left, which he did. Thinking to put him at ease, the examiner said, "Now settle down, you appear nervous, this is perfectly normal but it's affecting your gear changes, take your time and compose yourself and then drive on."

At this the candidate asked if he could have a bit of time to practice his gear changing.

"I'm afraid not, this is your driving test not a lesson, now drive on please"

"But I'm not used to a steering column gear change, my little Ford has a floor mounted lever"

"Then why did you come for your test in this car if you're not used to it?"

"I didn't come in this. It was outside the test centre, so I thought it was the car you use for testing people in."

This rather gob smacked the examiner, he collected his wits, stuffed his papers into a folder and said, "we'd better get this car back to where it was before anyone reports it stolen"

They returned it from whence it came, albeit rather jerkily and left it, fairly hurriedly, for the safety of the test centre.

I don't know what the outcome was but I'd like to have seen the owner's face when he came back and found his car on the opposite side of the road and facing in a different direction. He couldn't blame Jeremy Beadle for that!

。。🛈。。

The second event, 'round about this time, involved a motor cyclist. He presented himself for test with, not so much a sidecar attached to his bike, more a tool-box on a wheel. The tool-box was empty and an attempt had been made to fit a seat for the examiner in it.

In those days the examiner would relay his directions to the bike rider by a combination of hand signals and shouting above the noise of the engine, from the sidecar.

All went well until near the end of the test, the examiner asked the rider to take a rather sharp right hand turn. The message didn't get through until it was nearly too late. The rider tried manfully to make it but it was not to be. The severity of the late turn was too much for the couplings twixt bike and box. They parted company and although the bike and its rider managed to complete the turn, the box and passenger travelled diagonally across the junction which, fortunately, was devoid of traffic.

The speed in the single wheel saw it stay upright for most if its journey but by the time it got to the kerb it was running out of speed and the box and the examiner finished up in an undignified heap, half on and half off the footpath.

Chapter Seven
'L' IS FOR LEFT

Examiners come in for a lot of criticism, sometimes it is justified but usually it comes from test candidates who have just been told that their driving has not reached the required standard. Some examiners enjoy having something akin to a reputation. Most of them however are taking note of the mandates from the D.S.A. to be professional but at the same time, be friendly towards the candidates who will usually be wishing they were anywhere but where they are - taking a driving test.

After many years, during which they adopted a thoroughly domineering attitude, they have come round to acknowledging that without people to take tests, they wouldn't have the job of testing them.

A strange fact to emerge from this recent joining together of spirits, might give the examiners of bygone years a bit of sardonic satisfaction - it has done nothing to improve pass rates. The overall success rate fluctuates around the 50% mark all the time.

Attitudes may have lightened but bureaucracy has got heavier. Licences must be signed as soon as they are received. An unsigned licence means a cancelled test. Theory pass certificates must be shown, car insurance vouched for and photographic evidence must be produced to confirm you are who you say you are before the examiner will invite you to lead him out to your car.

In the time when a provisional licence was all the examiner required to see, an elderly lady was presented for test by her instructor who had neglected to ensure the provisional was signed. She showed it on request to her examiner who boomed, "Make it legal madam and sign it"

This did nothing for the poor dear's already frayed nerves.

"Oh dear, I hope you're not that horrid examiner my instructor told me about"

"And who might that be, did this instructor of yours give you a name for this horrid specimen?"

Guess what? He had. It was.

Her instructor was by this time deeply engrossed in a motoring magazine, trying to believe that this wasn't happening.

Shortly after this episode, the same A.D.I. was teaching a young man who was proving really hard work. After about 8 lessons he was just about to come to terms with the clutch. He mentioned that his Uncle was visiting them at the weekend from Harrogate and he'd told his nephew that he would take him out for some driving practice. Understandably the A.D.I. wasn't too keen on his pupil coming under someone else's influence, at what for him was still an early stage. Playing the situation down a bit he asked if Uncle did much driving?

"Yes he does a lot" answered the boy.

"In fact you might know him"

Guess what? He did, it was the horrid examiner who had recently found out, that that was the way he was referred to - by his nephew's driving instructor.

○ ○ 🄻 ○ ○

At all test centres there is a waiting room in which candidates sit chewing their nails or chomping on some chewing gum, with their instructors or whoever else brought them for their test. Exactly on time, the examiners emerge from their den and each one calls out the name of the eager beaver he or she is about to test.

A lady examiner told me of the occasion on which she was the first examiner to enter the waiting room. Immediately opposite her as she came in was a very buxom blonde whose cleavage was so low it left very little for the imagination.

The exact expression she used when telling me the tale was, "If I'd looked closer I'd have seen her bell —-navel"

It wasn't the blonde's lucky day. Out of 7 examiners she got the only lady.

As she heard her name being called out by this very feminine voice she gave a quick shrug of her shoulders and everything disappeared from view as quick as a flash.

○ ○ 🄻 ○ ○

Many test centres have car parks from which tests begin and end. We don't have such luxuries in Leeds. Our choice consists of the main road or a few side streets. At the main test centre, examiners always finish a test in a long straight side road which leads down to the local cemetery. Always that is, unless they require a sandwich from the nearby garage for lunch.

Examiners who smoke will take the candidate right to the end of the side road, not exactly into the cemetery but I'm sure they would if they could get a plot number. This gives them time to enjoy their king size on the longish walk back.

This test centre, Hillcrest House, is a large square grotesque building situated at the top of a hill, hence the name.

Before it became the grotty building it is now it used to be a tall elegant cinema, which I remember with affection, as I did a lot of my courting there. In fact my wife and I had our first date there. I don't think we said much after we sat down, a bit like the test candidates who enter it's re-constructed portals nowadays. We didn't say much, not for the obvious reason but she had brought with her a bag of sticky treacle toffee her mother had made that afternoon. A mouthful of that ensured two things, a visit to the dentist would be imminent and you were not going to get your jaws apart for some time to come. I've always been under the impression her mother knew what she was doing when her hand slipped as she added the treacle. At least we saw the film.

Occasionally we get requests to teach people to drive in their own cars. It saves wear and tear on our vehicle but of course the downside is we have no dual controls.

I recall one such course of lessons. Judy's mum and dad both drove the same car and it was their intention to take Judy out for practice when she reached a suitable standard. This would help her and probably save mum and dad a bob or two on lessons. Sounds like a good idea but Judy wasn't keen on it. She didn't want either of them 'teaching' her.

"They fight like cat and dog when they're driving, dad never does anything right for my mum and it's the same when she's driving, dad's always on at her"

She had two lessons a week, dad paid for one and her mum the other and I was to let them know as soon as she was doing well enough for them to take her out. Judy found concentrating very difficult and consequently her progress was slow. After 20 lessons I was still not happy to give her parents the go ahead, this of course suited Judy. Strangely after her 20th lesson she really started to make some good progress.

Some pupils appear to reach a watershed in their lessons where each one shows a marked improvement on the last one and this is what happened in Judy's case. She started to concentrate and be positive. Despite Judy's request I could no longer keep her parents at bay. She went with them both in turn over the next weekend. I saw her dad when I picked Judy up for her next lesson,

"She's all yours" He said and disappeared into the house.

I couldn't believe she could be so devious. She told me she had deliberately put the wind up them both in a variety of ways. They didn't make any more overtures and Judy eventually passed her test at her third attempt. Perhaps if she had got some practice with mum and dad she might have passed sooner.

Another 'own car' job again involved a car used by both parents. This time they were heavy smokers. As well as the overpowering smell of tobacco in the car, the front windscreen was almost opaque from the nicotine stains. We got through the first lesson and on our return, I asked as politely as I could, if I could clean the car windows. His dad thought I'd gone barmy and said I could do the whole car if I wanted. He soon changed his mind when I asked for a brillo pad and some scouring powder.

Incredibly they hadn't noticed the build up of gunge on the windows as they puffed merrily away during their driving hours. He was amazed when he saw it coming off the glass. I left him to it and although the pong was still there next lesson we could see where we were going.

I wrote about the following telephone conversation in the local newsletter so I can recount it almost verbatim. The man had a foreign accent and it wasn't always easy to understand all he said. Consequently I had to ask him to repeat himself several times, which made recalling it that much easier.

He started by introducing himself and then he asked how much I charged for lessons. Did I give a discount for block bookings? Could his wife sit in the back of the car during his lessons? What kind of car was it? Would he be taking his test in the same car? Would he have the same instructor for every lesson? He had driven a lorry in Iran about 6 years ago would that help? How many lessons did I think he would need to pass his test? Would I have any trouble in the car with his accent? Was there any colour bar at the test centre? Where was the test centre? And finally, what were British examiners like?

After I'd answered all his questions, he thanked me for my

patience and added, "I'm calling a number of instructors before I make a decision"

I didn't hear from him again and couldn't help wondering if it was the answer I gave to his last question that put him off.

Eddie, having got over hallucinating Karen, told me of a phone call he took from an elderly lady asking for a refresher course. She told him that she hadn't driven for some time but her husband wasn't well so she'd decided to make an effort. Eddie picked her up and was a bit surprised to find she was in her 70's. He drove to a quiet spot not far from the lady's house and they changed places. He asked to see her licence and while she searched for it in her tea chest size handbag, he asked when she had last driven.

"Not since I passed my test"

"When was that?"

"I can't remember the exact date but it was quite a long while ago. I do remember the car though, it was a Morris Minor. I had to bang on the side of it to make those signal things stick out, it was such a nuisance"

She eventually found her licence and though Eddie gave her an appraisal, it was more out of courtesy than expectation. They both agreed it would be best if she didn't pursue it further. 35 years is a long time to make up on a refresher course.

Those trafficators Eddie's lady referred to were usually reliable but if they did go wrong they could be a problem to get sorted out.

The following incident involved a friend of Bert, a colleague of mine. He had a van which relied on trafficators to let others know his intentions. The problem was they wouldn't retract after use. The right turning signal was not too difficult, that just required a sharp bang on the side of the van just behind the driver's right ear. To cancel the left signal was more difficult because of the width of the van. He carried a length of 2" x 2" timber for this purpose. A well directed jab with it usually did the trick.

Having turned left onto a main road on one occasion, he used his trusty lance to cancel the signal and carried on down the road. He was taken by surprise when a large car pulled out in front of him from a side street on his left. As collisions go it was quite gentle but nevertheless he left his mark on the large car's front wing. The driver of the car was in proportion to his vehicle. He got out, surveyed the damage and hot footed it to the van.

"You stupid ass, you're signalling left and you came straight on"

"I didn't signal, you came straight out"

"I came out because you signalled to turn in"

"No I didn't, it's your fault"

"You signalled, in fact you're signalling now"

"No I'm not"

At this the car driver wrenched the offending trafficator off the van and thrust it at its owner."Quite right, you're not signalling, now let me have your insurance details"

We should all know it's not a good thing to be vindictive while driving. Even so, there is a certain amount of satisfaction to be had, like the feeling you get when you find the driver who rushed passed you at a spot where he shouldn't, is waiting at the next set of lights as you cruise slowly up behind or alongside him, as if to say; "What's all the rush?"

I think it comes under the heading of 'come uppance'. The following item certainly does.

There is a long stretch of road that runs through a wood on my patch. I find it ideal for an early stage lesson involving starting, moving away and stopping. It isn't a particularly wide road and although the speed limit is 40, it suits this lesson admirably. On one occasion though it proved not so good.

Russ was only 17 but very big for his age. He had hands like shovels and big shovels at that. Although he was young enough to be my grandson, on lessons he gave the impression of being my minder.

We were going to do his starting and stopping session as the first half of this day's lesson. We entered the wooded road at one end and it was our intention to drive its length, about a mile and a half, pulling away, going up through the gears and stopping about 4 or 5 times before we reached the other end. Having parked up for the first time, we were aware of three youngsters on bikes, about 40 yards ahead of us. They appeared to be clowning around, riding slowly and swerving about.

We moved away from the kerb and Russ went into second gear. The three youths were aware of us by now and as we got nearer, they spread out across the road, effectively blocking our progress. Using the horn had no effect, so we had to move as slowly as they were going. An approaching lorry made them move over but as soon as it had gone they fanned out again. I felt sure that if we stopped, so would they, so we kept on the move.

Russ was all for stopping and sorting them out and tempting though this idea was, it wasn't really on. We had by now a convoy of about 5 honking cars behind us and one of them actually squeezed passed between two of the cyclists. We travelled like this for about a mile before we could turn off to the left. The only problem was that this turn took us onto roads that Russ wasn't ready for, so I took over and drove back through the streets to the start of the road we had just left. My reasoning was that the cyclists, having got rid of the learner, would begin to make normal progress and should be well away by the time we got to the other end.

We started to make good progress with our lesson and we were getting to the end of the road when we came across them again. This time they were coming towards us. We spotted them as we came round a bend onto a straight stretch of the road. They were not meandering now but they looked like the bottom tier of a motor-cycle display team. They were standing upright on their pedals with their arms locked around each other's shoulders. It would have looked rather impressive if it hadn't been taking place on a narrow 40mph road. Fortunately the road was quiet at the time but unfortunately for them, it was the one in the centre who saw us first. He must have forgotten they were all linked together. As soon as he saw our car and recognised the headboard he tried to point us out to his pals with disastrous consequences. His right arm only came over so far before he completely unbalanced all three of them.

They ended up in a tangled heap at the side of the road. As we drove past it looked like a cross between a fallen rugby scrum and a scrap yard.

I said to Russ, "Shall we stop and see if they are alright."

"Like hell we will, they had it coming."

I've never known whether 'hell' calls for a contribution to my swear box or not, so I said nothing — as I said, he's the minder.

Eric had been socialising on Sunday night, the necessary raw eggs and Alka Seltzer resulted in him leaving home on Monday morning 15 minutes late for his first pupil. She was very understanding apparently when he got there and explained about his flat tyre making him late. They got underway and the lesson had reached the half way stage when the police car pulled in behind them and followed along.

A police car behind somehow has the effect of making pupils develop a guilt complex.

"No, he's not following you for any misdeed you have committed, he's just on patrol" is my standard, hopefully soothing comment and probably Eric said something similar to his pupil. Five minutes later however, the Panda car was still behind them and by this time Eric was getting sticky under the collar.

"Brake lights" he thought, "I haven't checked my brake lights this weekend, - can't be those though, they'd have told me by now, come on someone, dial 999"

Eventually the police driver pulled alongside Eric and gestured to him to pull over. The Panda stopped in front of Eric's car and a WPC got out of the passenger side and walked back to him. "Good morning Sir, are you teaching this young lady to drive?"

"Yes officer"

"Shouldn't you be displaying 'L' plates?"

"I don't need 'L' plates when I've got my pod on"

"What's a pod?"

"My roof sign."

"Would you mind stepping out of the car Sir?"

"Not at all"

"Where is this 'pod'?"

Eric had what is called a flashback, he saw himself coming out of the house that morning 15 minutes late, the raw egg taste still in his mouth and he couldn't remember getting his pod out of the boot and putting it in place on the roof of the car. He hadn't, he stared at his bare roof. He's a bit of a charmer, or thinks he is!

"Sorry officer, it's been one of those mornings" he said pulling the pod out of the boot and fixing it in place,

"There we are, all complete, can we go?"
He got away with it, I don't think I would have.

In a previous existence before I became an A.D.I. I had a job which meant I was travelling an awful lot of miles, often more than 1000 miles a week and there was no time to hang about. I was stopped for speeding <u>three times</u> in a 4 year period and charged <u>three times</u>. A colleague of mine in the company was stopped 7 times in 5 years and wasn't charged once. His name was Murphy and although the furthest west he had been was Liverpool he used to say it was the luck of the Irish. I considered changing my name by deed poll by adding O' to my surname and seeing if some of that luck would rub off if I became O'Swift but have you seen how much they charge to change your name?

After passing Parts One and Two of the A.D.I. examination, I chose not to take out a Trainee licence. To have done so would have meant tying myself to a driving school for a considerable time. It wouldn't have needed to be a large school, often A.D.I.'s with more work than they can cope with, will take on a Trainee to cover the surplus work. Between them they can build on the original work and seek to expand the school. The experience gained should enable the Trainee to pass his Part Three. If he's happy with the situation and work continues to flow, he would then have the option of staying with the school or deciding to go on his own.

I decided I didn't want to be tied, so I made the choice to advertise locally for unemployed people to take FREE lessons, they could learn to drive while I gained experience as an instructor. The situation suited both parties. Although I can't recommend it to other 'would-be's' it worked for me.

I had plenty of offers and selected six pupils from a variety of backgrounds. I had no income and all my expenses to bear and that really concentrates the mind. Without a Trainee licence or a Part Three it is illegal to charge for lessons.

After qualification I was able to charge and my 6 guinea pigs stayed with me at a nominal fee. Five of them passed their tests, the other one left the area before she could do so.

Leafleting then brought me enough work to continue full time.

A.D.I.'s who decide to go on their own will usually carry a headboard on the car proclaiming the name of their school. Others will settle for 'L' plates at front and rear. I'm never sure why they choose to remain anonymous like this, I've heard some unflattering reasons mooted but I'm sure it's simply that they can't be bothered with a headboard. I feel they miss out on a good opportunity to advertise their school by not carrying one.

I've picked up quite a few 'cold' pupils through my yellow and red headboard. Having been involved in marketing in the years before I came into driving instruction. I fancied a different

"Don't you think you're taking your corporate image a bit too far Mr Swift.?"

appearance to the usual school image. To this end, I had a normal headboard painted yellow and had my name and phone number painted red. The same colour scheme I used on my pupil's progress sheets and my business cards.

As well as quite a few pupils my yellow headboard has brought me a rocket from a Senior Examiner and a bout of explaining to do to my wife.

Pupil-wise the number is unquantifiable because from anyone attracted to my school by the headboard I would expect to get referrals. This means that over a period of time the links between pupils and the origin of their particular chain become obscured. All I can say is, from memory, my headboard and it's painting cost me about £120. It has repaid that handsomely.

My rocket from the S.E. came at the time I presented my 6th pupil for his test. As the examiners and candidates were leaving the centre to go on test, the S.E. said in a loud voice, "Mr Swift would you stay behind after the test, I want a word with you"

He was totally out of order saying what he did in the way that he said it. He is quite within his rights to 'have a word' but not to announce it as though I was being kept in after school.

All sorts of advice was thrown at me by the other A.D.I.'s who could hardly conceal their delight and curiosity. At the end of the test I went to meet the S.E. as he walked back from my car, any feelings of anger were swept away by his opening words. "ah, Mr. Swift thanks for coming out and saving me a bit of time, I thought I'd have a word with you about a little matter before someone in a uniform does".

He then went on to tell me that my headboard, my stroke of marketing genius, was illegal. The 'L' must be on a white background which must be to certain specifications. *My* 'L' was on yellow. By the time he'd finished explaining everything I'd forgotten about his opening gambit in the waiting room. I just got in the car, took my pupil home, did two more lessons (with illegal headboard), bought a can of white spray paint, went home and sprayed around my "L' to the specifications I'd been given - and that was that, legal again.

The third problem 'old yellow' brought me involved a girl pupil, the girl's sister and my wife. Sounds a bit ominous, I'll call the girl Peggy. She was in her mid 20's, lived on the south side of the City and worked in the City centre.

I picked Peggy up for her lesson at 4pm from work. She had been a slow learner and town work was still fairly new to her. The lesson was planned so that she would work her way through the traffic in the general direction of home. When she'd settled into the car however she asked if I would mind if we picked her sister up during the lesson, as she was going with Peggy to their mother's for a meal. It didn't sound like a problem until she told me that her sister, Alice, lived just out of the City to the north in a well known red-light area.

I re-shaped the lesson so that we could make the pick-up.

Peggy had never been to her sister's house before and honestly, I didn't know the red-light area very well either. It took some time to find Alice but we eventually got there. By the time we arrived at their mother's the lesson had over-run by 20 minutes because of the delay finding Alice and the town traffic.

When I dropped them off, I was already 5 minutes late to pick my next pupil up. They both realised my problem and were overly apologetic for the inconvenience and overly grateful for what had in effect, been a taxi service.

By the time I finished work that night, I was nearly an hour late but my evening meal was still hot, the dust-bin was on fire!

About a week later, between lessons, my wife asked me to take her into town (does she think I'm a taxi?) A convenient way into town from where we live is through the red-light area. Don't get ahead of me here. It was early afternoon, the ladies of the night were starting their day shift. As we came up a hill, two short skirts in high heels were leaning against a wall in conversation. As we got nearer, I had to slow down for a sharp left turn onto the main road, one of them detached herself from the wall and tottered to the kerbside. As we went passed her, Alice bent down and said, "thanks again for the other night, John."

This gave me two problems, the first was immediate and the other one would come the next week. My wife has sharp elbows, in fact they are diamond hard. I've seen Martial Arts experts breaking piles of roof tiles with their heads or their elbows, no problem to my wife, she wouldn't even have to psyche herself up for it, BANG - it's done.

However we talked it through and decided divorce would be too expensive so we settled for a spot of mild to severe bruising of the ribcage.

The second problem was to come with Peggy's next lesson. Did she know how her sister earned her pennies? Should I just come out and say, "I saw Alice working the other day," hastily explaining that she wasn't working WITH me. Or do I say nowt and hope Alice didn't mention it either?

My pupils are always telling me I worry too much, as soon as Peggy got in the car she said, "Alice sends her apologies. I've to tell you she's sorry she called out to you the other day. You'd gone passed before she realised it could have been your wife in the car with you"

It didn't seem appropriate to show her my bruises but she obviously knew what her sister got up to when she wasn't having a meal at their mothers.

Since that incident I've tried to avoid the area. Should Alice be on duty again as we pass, I might have a bit of explaining to do to pupils if she's still feeling grateful.

It's usual for instructors to accompany their pupils into the test centre when presenting them for test. Normally we'd then wait in the test centre, chatting, probably pulling the examiners to pieces or we'd walk down to a nearby cafe, while the test took place.

Test centres now have drink machines as part of their hospitality up-grade. I don't drink coffee, however where these machines are concerned, everyone else does. As a result, when some poor soul wants to get a cup of tea out of this monolith in the corner, it's about three years since the last one was dispensed. Consequently it comes out looking like liquid rust and I can imagine it tasting like it as well so I pass on it and go to the cafe.

One A.D.I. in Leeds doesn't go into the centre with his pupils, I don't think it's because he's afraid someone will make him drink the tea, it's more that he is worried about his car when he can't see it. He waits in the car until the examiner and candidate come out to go on test and then he reluctantly gives up his vehicle and goes for a stroll. Strange behaviour and not really fair on his pupils who could, I'm sure, do with a bit of comfort at that time.

Another eccentric A.D.I. I know had a Ford Escort hatchback in which he used to teach. Reversing is not the easiest manoeuvre for a learner to pick up and it is even more difficult in the dark.

After all, it is a distinct advantage if you can see the kerb you are trying to follow. Our A.D.I. had it all thought out. He'd park the pupil up and tell them exactly what they had to do. Then he *got out* of the car, raised the tail-gate of the Escort and called directions through the open back of the car.

The pupil would be reversing in the dark to instructions such as - "Come on, clutch up a bit, straight back, whoa slow down, come on, come on NOW left hand down a bit, bit more, bit more, straighten up, clutch up a bit, get your steering wheel straight, slow down, that's fine, stop it there"

As an added teaching aid, on a really dark night he would hold a torch and shine it on the kerb to guide the now illegal pupil round it.

I have to report he no longer uses this method of instruction. Whether it's because he no longer has a car with a tail-gate I'm not sure, after all he could use an open rear window, no, I think the reason is that one of his pupils ran over his foot while he was trying to get his torch working.

Mick was in a car for the first time with the daughter of the very proud owner of a brand new, very large, very expensive motor. Although they were not short of a bob or two, father had made it clear to Mick that he didn't want to spend a lot on lessons. This was the reason Mick wasn't in his own car, dad was intent on taking over, teaching his daughter as soon as Mick had done the hard work. In order to get her moving and, in a way, to look after the car until she could handle such a beast, Mick had taken her to a disused airstrip outside Leeds.

So, there they were, lovely summer's day, windows right down, birds singing, engine purring away hardly making a sound, briefing done and a mile of runway stretching out in front of them as straight as an arrow. "O.K. then, clutch down, into first gear, mirror check, release the handbrake and come up nice and gently on the clutch. Wonderful, now just a little drop of gas and I'll tell you when to go into second gear"

The girl's a natural thought Mick as she responded to his instructions to go through the gears. They were cruising away in third gear and still no engine noise to drown the birds' singing. He was about to ask her for 4th gear when suddenly there *was* engine noise, a *lot* of engine noise. It wasn't coming from the front of the car, it was coming from above and behind.

A shadow passed over the car and as Mick looked up he saw a Tiger Moth training aircraft, passing overhead, but only just overhead, in fact he was overhead by no more than 20 feet!! The pilot was tipping the aircraft from side to side and from his days in the R.A.F. Mick understood the signal to mean, "I need to come in to land."

By this time they were more than half way down the runway so Mick used his right hand on the steering wheel to gently guide the car off the tarmac onto the grass.

"What are you doing?" asked his pupil.

"That aircraft needs to come in to land"

"Well surely there's plenty of room for both of us without having to go off the road, we're supposed to be having an hour's lesson, we've only been here 10 minutes."

Mick had a mental picture of her dad's face as he looked at his flash car with a Tiger Moth jammed on it's roof.

Everything turned out right, Tiger Moths don't require much runway, the girl got her full hour and Mick? Well, Mick just enjoyed being in the car.

"I've paid for an hour and that's what I'm going to have!"

Laurie like Mick has been teaching people to drive since before cars were invented, or so it seems. He had a pupil on lesson about to do her first turn-in-the-road manoeuvre. She was only young and a mad keen horse rider, own pony, gymkhanas the lot.

Laurie had told her what he wanted her to do and she set off across the road in first gear, good control and nice progressive braking but she stopped too short of the kerb to satisfy Laurie so he urged her to go a bit further.

She would have needed to have raised the clutch pedal slightly and just eased off the brake for a moment or two. Instead, keeping both clutch and brake to the floor, she raised herself up slightly and went "clic clic" as though she was urging her pony on.

Although she blushed, she took it in good part when Laurie explained that horse power and horses don't speak the same language.

I spoke earlier about the petrol shortage caused by the Egyptian conflict and how it enabled Learner drivers to drive unaccompanied. I took my driving test during that period and I remember part of it very well.

I was in business and used a van to ferry stock around. I'd been doing this for about 10 weeks when it was brought to my notice that to do this legally I required a 'C' licence. What the initial stood for, unless it was Carrier, I've no idea.

I applied for a 'C" licence, after all I looked upon myself as a law abiding citizen. The 'C' Licence came through the letter box on the morning of my driving test. Was this an omen? 'C' licences didn't have to be displayed anywhere rather like a driving licence you just have to have one.

This 'omen' business intrigued me so I decided, naively, to lay the licence on the dashboard where the examiner could see it and think 'this young man needs to pass his test to help keep his business going'.. 'Yeerk'!! So I arrived at the test centre with my ace-in-the-hole laid as conspicuously as it could be on the dashboard.

We set off on the test, up the hill towards Leeds University. I noticed a youngish girl, on one side of the road, probably a student, with her head buried in a book walking towards a pedestrian crossing. As we got nearer, she glanced up from her book and saw a bus coming down the hill towards us, obviously her bus, she burst into a sprint and hurtled onto the crossing. I had to slam the brakes on and we stopped just off the crossing and barely a yard from her as she cut across in front of us. Phew, the examiner hauled himself back into his seat, no seat belts then, and said, "strewth, you know where she was going?" Meaning I suppose, the bus stop.

"She was going to hospital if I'd hit her."

It was a warm day made considerably warmer by that incident but the rest of the test went off uneventfully. The examiner was kind enough to pass me and said he hadn't felt it necessary to ask me for another emergency stop after the episode, I had to confess that I hadn't noticed. He also said, "by the way, I hope that bit of paper that blew out of the window as you brought the van to a stop for the young lady, wasn't important!!

I waited a week to see if it was handed in to the police but, no luck, so I had to apply for another 'C" licence, whatever it stood for. Serves me right for trying to be devious.

What is it about driving that makes normal sensible people become confused as to which is their left and which is their right? Most of them have it sorted by their 5th or 6th lesson but even *they* make the odd mistake later on. When it comes to reversing we find the problem starting all over again. For some people this is a *serious* problem and has nothing to do with driving - but I'm thinking here of the learner driver who has had no problem for the last umpteen years distinguishing their left side from t'other and as we come to a junction, on the instruction, 'look right, left and right,' find themselves craning forward to look *left*!

There won't be a driver who, on their first turn-in-the-road manoeuvre, at the start of the reverse element didn't look over their *right* shoulder after being told to look over the left one. I'm sure I was the same. I think it's in-bred obstinacy.

I won't be the only A.D.I. to have written 'L' and 'R' on my pupil's hands.

I did hear of an instructor who hung a Rabbit key ring on the Right side of her windscreen and a Lion key ring on the left side. Her instructions contained phrases like, "we'll take the second road on the rabbit please." Barmy, but you do get a bit desperate. She didn't use the key rings for *all* her pupils I'm assured.

One 17 year old girl had this problem a little more than normal and we'd spend the first few minutes of each lesson doing simple exercises to get her mind focused on left and right. It didn't fully solve the problem but this apart, she was a good driver. Funnily enough, when she was reversing she had no problem telling which was which. We noted her problem on her test application form and the examiner treated her in a similar way he would a deaf person - by pointing.

"This is your left hand and this........."

Chapter Eight
THE PLEASURES OF COLDITZ

Occasionally pupils ask their instructor to sit-in with them on their test. Why they want this to happen, is never made quite clear. Some say it will give them confidence, others feel they will be sure of a fair test if an A.D.I. is there to 'keep an eye on the examiner'. If a pupil fails a few tests then it might be a good idea for an instructor to suggest sitting-in to see just what is going wrong.

A.D.I.'s are welcome, indeed encouraged, by most examiners to sit-in. It's a revelation sometimes to watch our pupils driving in a manner that can be completely alien to the way they have been doing for so long on lessons. We sit back, not allowed to do or say anything that could be construed as help to the candidate. Afterwards we are asked if we have any comment to make on how the test was conducted or about the examiner's debrief.

During the debrief, the examiner will tell a failed candidate why and where they failed. If the candidate passed. then, if he had a persistent minor fault, this would be pointed out and he would be given a sheet with his minor faults marked on.

If things go well during a sit-in then it's an enjoyable experience but on the other hand it can be quite horrendous.

It is very difficult to resist looking over your shoulder when your pupil is about to emerge from a junction. One gets so used to doing it on lessons that it is a natural instinct but it could be interpreted as a reminder to the driver.

A driving school I know well has a male and female instructor making up its total strength. The lady instructor sat-in on a test in the early part of one week and was seen by the examiner to make an instinctive glance over her shoulder at a junction. The examiner mentioned this to her afterwards telling her she should not have done it.

Later in the week, her partner was sitting-in and by coincidence, got the same examiner. On the way to the car, the examiner, foolishly, mentioned the earlier incident and said quite forcibly that he didn't want a repetition of it. This of course, struck a nerve with the A.D.I. and a letter of complaint was sent to the Senior Examiner asking for an apology. This was forthcoming and the incident was forgotten.

Before the advent of the Extended Theory Test, the examiner would test a candidate's knowledge of the Highway Code by asking a selection of randomly chosen questions after the practical test.

One A.D.I. who wished he hadn't sat-in, heard his pupil, a sweet old lady, answer the question 'What would you be aware of while passing a line of parked cars?' with, "blood and sudden death" and to the question, 'what are the principal causes of skidding? , she replied, 'orange peel and banana skins.' Where she got those answers from, no-one knows.

A pupil asked me fairly early on in her lessons if it was true that I could accompany her on her test."Yes" I said, "in fact anyone can sit with you, providing they say nowt and keep out of your eyeline during your manoeuvres"

So it was arranged, I'd sit-in with her on her test. She confirmed this two lessons before the day. Next lesson she asked if I minded if she changed her mind.

"No I don't mind but why?"

"I'd like my mother to sit with me"

I'd taught her mother to drive about two years previously and I remembered the state she'd been in before she took her test. I'd had to stop off and get her some chewing gum, her mouth had dried so much. Her left leg was nearly uncontrollable in the hour before and on the way to the test centre she'd been like a jelly. Five minutes into her test the examiner had parked her up and asked her to settle down. She had actually passed her test but only heaven knows how, the state she was in. These memories suggested to me that this wasn't the best idea I'd heard that week.

I asked Andrea if she was certain about this and was her mother in agreement?

"Yes" and "Yes" - so her mother came too.

Andrea passed her test and was quite composed beforehand but her mother was again in a dreadful state. She needed more chewing gum and asked me if the examiner would object to pulling up if she didn't feel well again.

How Andrea could put her mother through those agonies, I'll never know.

I sat-in on two tests in one week at different centres. On the first, my pupil failed on one point. The examiner thought he shouldn't have entered a roundabout when he did. I thought he was quite safe and had plenty of time. On the second test, my pupil drove very well, except I thought he entered a roundabout when he should have given way. The examiner passed him. Thinking he had forgiven the roundabout error - because the rest of his driving had been so good, I mentioned the incident to the examiner afterwards, because had it been a lesson, I would have made him wait, but the examiner said, "oh, we'd let them get closer than that." Such are the vagaries of driving tests!

Pupils sometimes complain about being unjustly treated by examiners. When we sit-in and see for ourselves incidents like the two I witnessed in the one week, it is clear there is room for improvement still.

Ideally if a candidate was to pass a test with one examiner then they should pass with them all but this degree of consistency will never be achieved. Just as instructors are all individuals, teaching the same thing in their own way, then examiners are all individuals judging things in their own way and no amount of training will take away an individuals opinion. On the whole though, I do feel examiners get it right more often than not and we are going to have to settle for that.

It usually benefits a pupil to get some experience with someone other than their instructor when they are capable. This capability must take into account the fact that this third person will not have dual controls. As well as practice it gives them the benefit of having someone else alongside other than the familiar A.D.I. before they have the unfamiliar examiner.

Consequently, as soon as I feel they are ready to give someone this thrill, I'll give them the nod and suggest where they might go for this first exciting venture.

Kelly was due to go out with her dad for the first time at the weekend. I suggested a route for them which would keep them on fairly quiet roads and keep them reasonably near home. Came the next lesson.

"How did you get on with your dad?"

"Don't ask." But I did, I need to know, it's my job.

"Take the next on the left and park up as soon as you can and give me the gory details".

She told me they had limped round the course I'd set them but she stalled once or twice. Dad got a bit aerated and the final straw came at a junction about a quarter of a mile from home. In her words..
"I stalled it because someone shot across in front of me, then I stalled again and again"

By this time apparently her dad was stalled as well. He got her to roll the car down the hill through the junction, he then got out, took the keys and walked home, leaving the poor kid in the car to await her mother who was detailed to got and fetch her home.

Later, her mother told me, he'd got so uptight with Kelly stalling the car so much he didn't stop to think, it didn't occur to him to DRIVE the car home, he just stormed off.

"He's a bit like that" she added.

Eventually Kelly had the last laugh, her dad had needed three attempts to pass his test. Kelly did it in one. She now has a large company car and drives all over the country.

What Kelly's dad didn't allow for was the difference in the feel of the car to early stage drivers. The pedals feel quite different, the gear lever and even the seats have a strange feel compared to the ones in the car they are used to. It takes a bit of time to adjust to their new environment and though Kelly's dad was a very intelligent chap, he didn't use his common sense.

While on the subject of dads, I'm sometimes asked why their sons (It always seems to be sons) require so many more lessons than they themselves did. Assuming their memories are reliable, they seem to remember 'only having a dozen or so - and yet Tim has already had 18 and not put in for his test yet!'

They might not know, despite the publicity given to it, that the test has changed over the past few years and is somewhat more involved than it used to be in their day.

What they *should* realise however, is that our roads are considerably busier than they were 10 or 12 years ago. The increase in traffic has brought a corresponding increase in irresponsible driving and unfortunately this has resulted in the modern disease of 'Road Rage". Trying to avoid traffic jams and explaining the need to keep calm takes up a proportion of lesson time.

Ever since the second car came on the road, the potential for road rage has existed. Over the past few years it has grown terribly and with awful consequences at times. As with all diseases, prevention is better than cure and it is part of our job to make new drivers aware of the dangers of road rage.

I have to say that the smart ass media person who came up with the alliterative expression 'ROAD RAGE' has done no-one any favours. By giving bad tempered driving a snappy title, media man has tended to make it sound fashionable. Not long ago, a shake of the head would have been sufficient to register your opinion of a careless act by another driver. It has now got to the stage where even that mild rebuke could result in dire consequences.

"*I think he wants us to move!*"

As the roads get busier, tempers could get shorter, so action must be taken sooner rather than later.

Mick told me of the time he was struggling to teach a Polish lady who spoke some English but didn't always understand what she was saying nor did she always comprehend what was said to her. As Mick had no Polish whatsoever they had to get by as best they could.

She was in her 60's and as is so often the case with people that age, very set in her ways. Add to this and the language difficulties, the fact that she was 'Continental' in her outbursts when things didn't go as smoothly as they might, which was often. The Continental attitude was reflected by the fact that she tended to talk with her hands as much as with her mouth.

Mick spent a long time during her early lessons trying to impress on her it is not a good idea to take both hands off the wheel to gesticulate in order to make a point. However his real problem came when after about a dozen lessons the dear lady thought that because she could now change gear and turn corners she should be applying for her test. Not soon - but NOW.

Despite Mick proving to her she wasn't yet a driver, she persisted. It got to the stage where he wasn't looking forward to her lessons and more ear-bashing. It was at a time when he couldn't really pick and choose, he needed the work. So in order to keep her quiet during lessons, he let her apply for her test knowing there was a 12 week wait. The date come through, sure enough it was 12 weeks away. She was having two lessons a week so he consoled himself with the thought she might just be ready. But pigs can't fly and as the day came nearer it was plainly obvious to Mick that she wasn't going to be anywhere near. Unfortunately it wasn't obvious to the pupil.

He suggested they postpone the test but she wouldn't hear of it. It is clear in hindsight that by this time Mick should have withdrawn the use of his car. It is in his terms and conditions that he could do so, if he felt she was going to be unfit to test. Mick's a quiet person, she was a very strong character and although he'd never admit it, I think he must have been a bit scared of her, otherwise how would they end up at the test centre at the prescribed time to take the test?

That particular test centre is now closed and has been for some time. One of the reasons it was closed was its lack of accessibility. Examiners and instructors alike called it 'Colditz Castle' it was quite an appropriate name as it was very difficult to get away from and stood on a hill.

In the week leading up to the test Mick had worried himself silly trying to think of ways to stop this lady taking her test, nothing worked, the woman was adamant, she was going to take the test.

"I can drive, I've paid my money, why should I not take my test? What are you frightened of, that I will prove you wrong? Don't worry you have taught me well"

They had taken the unusual step of parking outside the Colditz car park, Mick had decided on this action in order to save the lady having to emerge from the difficult car park exit. They were in the waiting room and it was almost dead on the dot when either inspiration *came* or nerve *went*. Mick excused himself saying he wanted to visit the toilet. He went outside and using his spare key, he hi-jacked his own car. He drove away and out of Mrs Poland's life forever. He expected to hear from her demanding an explanation for his extreme action but not a word.

He did however hear from the Senior Examiner. He was asked, no he was ordered by way of a telephone call, to show himself at the S.E.'s office the next morning at 9.30 sharp. He was there on the dot. The S.E. met him outside the office and led him inside. Mick's car keys were laid on a table in front of him as he entered the office and he followed orders to sit down. The thought struck him that the keys looked ominously like a sword on a court martial table.

"Do you mind telling me what led to this unprecedented action of yours yesterday?"

"I didn't think the lady was fit to take her test but she simply wouldn't listen to me. I didn't think it fair to put one of your examiners in danger"

"My examiners are perfectly capable of looking after themselves and this sort of thing must never happen again." He went on, grinding it out, finally closing by saying, he was now going to have to write an explanatory letter to the lady.

He gave Mick his keys and bade him leave. As Mick left the office he heard the S.E. jingling his own keys in his pocket . For a long time after that, whenever Mick attended Colditz for a test, that was the way he was greeted by the examiners - and one or two quietly told him they wished more instructors would do a runner.

On another occasion Mick had reason to rue going to Colditz. He was sitting in on a test.

It had been fine and sunny during the pre-test hour but during the test it started to rain. It started lightly but got progressively heavier. The candidate didn't put the windscreen wipers on and it became increasingly difficult to see. The driver was obviously having trouble seeing because he was leaning forward and peering through the raindrops. The examiner turned round to Mick and said in a slightly sarcastic tone,

"Are your wipers working?"

The driver didn't realise the examiner was addressing Mick and said, "no, she's at home with the kids"

Mick was thoroughly fed-up with his pupil by this time and rasped, "he didn't ask after your *wife*, now put your bloody wipers on and we can see where we are going"

He wasn't actually working when the following incident occurred. He'd been parked at a meter in the City Centre on market day. Meters are valuable bits of real estate on market days as you can imagine. Mick was about to pull away, when a car came past on his right and took up a position to reverse into Mick's space as soon as he'd vacated it.

Another car driver, seeing Mick start to pull out, stopped behind him obviously intent on also pulling into the space. The driver in front, seeing the second car taking up its position, backed up a few metres preventing Mick pulling out. He left his car and walked past Mick and stopped level with the other car's front windscreen, he looked at it and then moved round so that he could speak to the driver.

Mick heard him say,"I'm sorry, I didn't realise you're a disabled driver"

"I'm not"

"You bloody well will be if you pinch my parking space".

During tests, examiners are required to give clear and understandable directions. However clear those directions are they are sometime misinterpreted. Usually this is because of nerves, although there might have been some other distraction.

Nerves play a large part in a candidate's performance and although approaching and emerging at junctions is probably the main practical reason for test failures, more tests will be failed because the candidate's nerves let them down. Making a minor mistake will not cost anyone their test but worrying about that minor mistake may cause them to make more mistakes and possibly these might be more serious. Once a mistake has been made it cannot be unmade so it is pointless worrying about it, concentrate on the remainder of the test and try and keep it fault free.

Candidates often take wrong turnings, providing everything is kept safe, this won't count against them.

A pupil of mine took three successive wrong turnings. Twice when asked to turn right, she went left and when asked to take a road to the left at a roundabout, she went ahead. The examiner asked her to pull up on the left and to make sure she did, he pointed LEFT. Anne managed this correctly. The examiner could see that she was desperately nervous and asked her to take minute or two to settle down.

He told her he didn't live in Leeds and he only knew the test routes. With all her meandering she'd gone off the route and he was now lost.

"Drive past that road on the left, park up and reverse into it and we'll go back the way we came and pick up the test route again"

Anne did this, they got back on track and incredibly, despite her lack of navigational skills, she passed her test - she had kept everything safe. I imagine she would be able to dine out for a few weeks on that story.

The following incident took place in an area of Leeds not used for driving tests now and it involved one of Cliff's more thoughtful pupils.

The test had been in progress for about 15 minutes when the examiner said to his young candidate, "stop at the next convenient place"

The boy looked at the examiner and after a quick check in his mirrors speeded up. After about a quarter of a mile he pulled into the kerb and stopped the car rather abruptly.

"There you are Sir," he said, pointing to the left.

He had been under the impression the examiner had been taken short and had pulled up outside the local public toilets!

I've often heard it said 'There is no such thing as bad publicity.' I can't be sure it's true but to build a business there must be some form of publicity. Most A.D.I.'s going on their own will have a name for their school. Many use an area name, others will use a set of initials. Many more, use their own name which really personalises them.

Joe is a friend of mine, he is not a driving instructor but it was in this connection that he phoned me from the South Coast one evening. He was working there for a while. That day he had seen a headboard on a driving school car which had made him do a double take. There are many schools with catchy names, some of them are quite humorous and others refer to motoring matters involved with tuition.

When Joe told me what he had seen, my initial reaction was the same as his had been - to cringe. Then I thought about it again. Joe had seen it and taken the trouble to call me to tell me about it, so it had obviously made an impression on him as it did on me. It would certainly stick in the mind of anyone in the vicinity thinking about driving lessons.

That's what advertising is all about, reminding people about your product. The name Joe saw is a fairly common surname and although it does have unfortunate connotations, I'll bet the locals remember it when they want lessons. Nice one, Mr Pratt of 'Pratt's Driving School'

We've had some peculiarly named schools over the years but I'd better go not further down that track, it could lead to libel action but I ask you, *'Crash Corsa?!'*

..🚗..

Cliff told me about Diane, a pupil of his, who became caught up with a funeral cortege while on the test. Diane had only been driving about 5 minutes when they caught up with the procession shortly after it left the church bound for the cemetery.

The road was narrow and there was no room for her to pass, so she had to tag along behind. By the time the road widened out, Diane had other cars behind her, the drivers of which re-acted quicker than she did to the opportunity to pass the procession. There would still have been time for her to pass however before the road narrowed again but she didn't. Through the narrow road they went, still processing and by now she had got herself into a bit of a rut, because she refused the chance to pass as the road widened out again. Eventually the cortege turned off to the left and Diane was at last able to make progress.

She told Cliff afterwards that by now she thought she'd blown it and sure enough the examiner had to fail her for 'undue hesitancy! As they drove home. Diane remembered what the examiner had said to her after passing his verdict. "Was the deceased a very close relative then?"

○ ○ 🗏 ○ ○

Dawn was going to New Zealand to spend a year with a friend on a farm. It would be convenient for her to have a driving licence to take with her. The distances between farms in rural N.Z. aren't exactly measured in light years but they are not next door either and she would have a car available. So Dawn had her lessons but failed her first test. The time for her departure was getting closer. The second test was now two days away and it snowed.

Even a light covering of snow means candidates might have difficulty seeing hazard warning lines as they approach junctions and emergency stops could take them into the next county, so inevitably, snow means cancellation of hostilities. Her flight to the other side of the world was now only two weeks away. The date for her re-arranged test came through, it was three days before she was due to leave the country.

That year, tests were cancelled only twice because of snow. The second bout of snow fell the day before Dawn's re-arranged test. It was cancelled, an urgent phone call to the booking office found her a spot for a test the day before she was due to fly. The proviso of course was that the snow cleared, it did, she passed and had her licence forwarded to her in New Zealand.

Talk about cutting it fine. I remembered all those years back when I'd hoped to appeal to the examiner's better instincts by displaying my 'C' licence on the dashboard. I was about to suggest that Dawn do the same with her flight tickets but then I remembered what happened to my 'C' licence. It flew out of the window.

"If this weather gets any worse we'll have to abandon the test."

Chapter Nine
FRUSTRATION AND FOREIGN TRAVEL

As with most professions, ours is not without it's frustrations. At the start of a course of lessons it's frustrating for both parties when a pupil finds it difficult to get the car moving owing to a lack of co-ordination between hands and feet. At the other end of the course, the main source of puzzlement comes when 'dead certs' go down. 'Dead certs' are pupils who you feel can't fail their test. How foolish! It is amazing how often these people do fail and yet others, who have the ability to pass but are often, to say the least, a bit up and down depending on mood swings, sail through.

It's difficult sometimes to convince pupils that it wasn't the examiner who failed them but, because he or she didn't do the job properly, they failed themselves. Prior to the test we often have to persuade pupils that examiners are not ogres. We do our best in this direction but still people come back, having failed saying, "he didn't like me from the start, I could tell"

"Why did he take this instant dislike to you?"

"I don't know, he just did"

Sometimes it takes a bit of tongue biting to avoid saying, "I don't blame him, it took me a while to get used to that meat hook you've got dangling from your ear."

How a candidate dresses should make no difference, which is just as well in a lot of cases!

An 18 year old girl I was teaching looked perfectly normal at the start of her lessons. At the end of her third she asked if I would mind if she wore make-up at her next lesson. I presumed she was going out at the end of it so I told her I didn't. She had already had some lessons before coming to me.

I'd forgotten about this until I arrived to pick her up. Jeepers creepers, my mother never told me about Goths....

Until she spoke, I couldn't tell it was the same girl. She had drip white make-up all over her face, black lipstick, black eye make up and spiky hair.

I'd all on not to burst out laughing but it didn't seem the correct thing. I got the impression she wanted me to say something, so I said the first thing that came to me. "Drive on when you're ready, we're going to practice clutch control"
We didn't half get some funny looks while waiting for traffic lights to change. It would have been interesting to have taken her to the test centre but she only had another half dozen lessons after that. Her grandmother in Dorset became ill and she had to go and look after her. I do hope she didn't burst in on Granny with that war-paint on.

One of my pupils had the start to her test delayed rather unusually. As she was walking to the car with the examiner, an egg was thrown from a passing car. It struck the examiner just below the knee, spattering his lower trouser leg with the sticky mixture you get from a broken egg. He had to return to his office to clean up before setting off again.

He's a good sort and laughed it off but I'll bet he took the first opportunity to check his previous days failures, just in case he got any of them again in the hope that he could have the last laugh.

As you would expect, learner drivers exhibit all the characteristics there are to be found in a cross section of the general public. Some are stoic and humourless and it's not a lot of fun teaching someone who makes no effort to be, at least, pleasant. Others are totally the opposite, seeing fun in every situation. Even this can become a bit wearing but they are infinitely preferable to the stoics.

It wouldn't be very interesting if we were all alike. 3 or 4 hours in the car with either extreme could be a toil of a pleasure. Fortunately the majority of people fit nicely in between these two types of personality. Give me Mr. or Mrs. Average any time.

It is a source of amazement to me how often I go through a course of lessons with a youngster and never see either of their parents. It's very nice to feel they trust me and don't feel the need to interrogate me before I drive off with their kids. We learn of children being attacked nearly every day from the newspapers and T.V. and I don't think it would go amiss, or be taken the wrong way, if parents were to run the rule over an instructor, particularly if he is a stranger to the family.

There are exceptions of course, some mums and dads are in the habit of asking for progress reports and these are the ones who are usually looking of the opportunity to take their off-spring out in the family car for some practice when they are ready.

One girl's mother who I'd seen regularly when I picked her daughter up for lessons, appeared at the test centre shortly after Kim had started her test. She spotted me with the other A.D.I's and came over and apologised for being late. I was slow on the uptake and said, "you're not late Kim isn't back yet"

"No I know, I was supposed to be here before she set off but I got delayed at work"

Before I could say anything she looked round and enquired where the other parents were. She was under the impression *all* parents made an effort to be there with their kids on test day. Apart from Andrea's mother, who had been there under duress, Kim's mother was the only parent of a pupil of mine who made the effort. In all honesty, I don't think too many children would want their parents turning up. Kim had kept quiet and not told me her mother was coming - probably in the hope that she wouldn't.

Nerves come into play an awful lot when someone is learning to drive. They affect people in different ways and I've known people give up because they feel they can never conquer their nerves.

Athletes say they need to be nervous to perform at their best. If this is the case why can't nervous people perform at their best behind the wheel? In early lessons they are attempting something they have never done before, so possibly the strangeness of what they are doing makes them afraid to look stupid. As they progress, some of the nerves will disappear but they come back at test-time. On this occasion it is because the person sitting next to them is judging their performance.

By the time pupils go for test, they should be capable of passing it and they must draw upon this knowledge to help get them through. I admire anyone who passes a driving test in today's road conditions. I often say, I wouldn't like to be learning to drive today.

The following two stories are my attempt to illustrate how nerves can affect people at varying stages of driving tuition.

Pupil: "Why do I put myself through all this self inflicted torture? Look at me, I'm a bag of nerves, I can't keep my legs still"
A.D.I.: "Don't worry, I know you blew it last time, put it behind you and concentrate on *this* attempt. You know you can do it, just hold yourself together and give it your best shot".
Pupil: "O.K. I promise I'll try, I hate letting you down, you've been so nice about it. Come on then, let's see what I can do"
A.D.I.: "That's the spirit, I've got every confidence in you"
Pupil: "It's L970 OUB - I did it, I did it. Oh I'm so pleased. Now can we start driving lessons?"

It was his first driving test after hours and hours of training. In retrospect it seemed like months and months. At last he was in the test centre thinking, 'I hope he'll go easy on me.'
What was it he had been told many times during his training? Be positive, be in control, hold yourself together for 30 minutes and it will be all over. It will pass quickly.

His knuckles gleamed white as he clenched and unclenched his fists in an effort to relieve the tension. His mouth was dry and his stomach was full of butterflies performing Swan Lake. The clock seemed to have slowed down as it approached 8.40. The first test of the day - in fact the first test of the week.

'Come on, come on, let's get it over with. Do I look the part?'

He'd put his best suit on for the occasion. 'No need for that extravagance,' he thought as he looked round him.

'God the tension, it must be 8.40 by now'
The door opened, the blood drained from his face. 'Why am I doing this to myself?' he wondered as the butterflies grew in size. He stepped forward and heard himself saying....

"Mr Young, would you sign here please and can I see your Theory pass certificate and your driver's licence?"

Lamp-posts, telegraph poles and trees can be a bit intimidating to pupils about to perform a turn-in-the-road manoeuvre, or as it is more commonly known, a three point turn, so if they can avoid parking by them, I'd get them to do so. My standard explanation regarding lamp-posts used to be: 'If you knock one of those over the Council will bill you for £300 to put it back up again.' I don't know where I got the figure from, it just seemed a reasonable amount for a concrete pole with a bit of wire running through it to a bulb on top.

Dorothy is the wife of an ex-footballing friend of mine, who used to be a driving instructor in a small town outside Leeds. They met when she became a pupil of Erics. Eric had ceased to be an instructor in favour of something more lucrative and Dorothy hadn't taken a test. She was now about to make her first turn-in-the-road for a few years. I gave her a full briefing and at the end I added my bit about the lamp-post. When I told her about it costing £300 to re-plant it, she rounded on me and hollered. "They charged me nearly £1000 !"

"You didn't" says I,

"I did," says she, "why do you think Eric stopped teaching me?"

"What happened?"

"I was turning into our drive and I only seemed to give it a nudge but it came down in pieces in the garden, it hardly marked the car but it didn't do Eric's roses much good"

My 'friend' hadn't told me that when he called to say,"I've got a job for you".

It's surprising how many people fail to turn up for their driving test. The examiners at my local test centre put 10p in a box every time they get stood up and by Christmas they've usually got enough to buy themselves a good night out. The amount of money wasted by candidates not turning up must pay quite a few bills for the D.S.A. in re-test fees.

Termination of tests take place far more often than one might think. If a candidate is driving dangerously, the examiner is quite within his right to stop the test. He would then remove the car keys and *walk* back to the test centre and hand them over to the person who accompanied the failed candidate, no doubt with a few well chosen words, especially if it was pouring with rain. He would explain where he had left the poor unfortunate and then fill in a termination report.

I've had two tests terminated and it's an awful experience. The first came about simply because my pupil ran the car into a lamp-post. No, it didn't come down and cost her 1000 quid but it did that amount of damage to my car. The examiner wasn't best pleased either, he didn't get whiplash in the normal place, he got it where it raised his voice by a couple of octaves. My pupil was in her 60's and although she had been very hard work at the start of lessons, she had developed into quite a good driver. O.K., I know good drivers don't usually finish a driving test half way up a lamp-post but there was a reason, not an excuse but a reason.

When her husband was alive she had never given a thought to driving, he'd always enjoyed it so she left it to him. When he died, she was lost. Outside in the drive was their Volkswagen Golf Gti, she could sell it or learn to drive it. She chose the latter because she thought it would be a form of therapy as well as being practical.

We started lessons, she was a very nice lady but absolutely hopeless in her co-ordination. Right from the start however, she found she enjoyed driving. We worked at it, twice a week and she improved. As she became more proficient, I took her out in the Golf a few times and she became confident enough to let driving friends sit with her to gain some practice and experience. Eventually she was driving them all over at weekends culminating in a trip to the Lake District.

She took her first test and failed it in the last 5 seconds. The examiner told me it had been a smashing drive but she didn't use her mirrors as she came in to park at the end of her test and there had been a string of vehicles behind her.

Shortly before her second test she was ill and missed lessons for the two weeks immediately before her test. She didn't want to postpone it and because she was so capable I didn't argue. What she didn't tell me until a couple of weeks later was she had taken two tablets a friend gave her to pep her up a bit after her illness. She did this just before I picked her up. She was fine during the pre-test lesson but they must have had an effect on her as she started her test. Rather than pep her up however, they had the opposite effect and slowed her reactions down. Going into a right hand turn she was too slow with her steering and had an argument with a lamp-post.
I'm not here to preach but be very careful what you put inside your body, especially if you intend driving.

My second termination was a strange affair. The examiner and my pupil had been gone about 20 minutes when the examiner appeared again in the waiting room. It was not a good thing for me to see. That man should still be in *my* car with *my* pupil on test, what the devil is he doing *here?* Shades of my car half way up a lamp-post flashed through my mind.

"Your indicators have packed up"

First thought – 'Phew is that all'.

He'd asked her to park up for the first manoeuvre and nothing had come on when she indicated left to pull in.

"Did you try them?" I asked him. He had and the lights and the horn and nothing was working electrically.

I took the keys and headed off to where he'd left the car and pupil. As luck would have it, another A.D.I. was passing as I left the test centre and he gave me a lift to my car. My pupil put her fag out and repeated what the examiner had told me as I got in. When I turned the ignition on, the left indicator which must have been switched on, came on. I tried the other it worked, the lights worked, the horn worked, and the hazard flashers, there was nothing wrong.

We zipped back to the test centre and I explained to the examiner but by now it was too late to continue the test. We booked another one two days later and she passed uneventfully. I had to pay for the re-booked test because the serviceability of my car is my responsibility. I had the electrics checked out and nothing could be found to cause the malfunction and it hasn't happened again. I don't believe in U.F.O.'s but don't they have this effect on cars in films?

░░🕮░░

I am often asked if women are as good as men when it comes to learning to drive. Without sitting on the fence, I would say on average there is very little difference. Both sexes have their exceptions where learning either comes quickly or particularly slowly. The majority of people learning to drive are young (well they *are* compared to me) and young boys are usually more curious about the car and how it works than girls, particularly when it comes to how fast it will go.

The main feature of anyone's learning curve is the frequency of lessons. From experience, I would estimate that a person taking only 1 lesson per week will require up to half a dozen more lessons than someone who is taking two or more a week.

If girls do have an obvious weakness, it is probably a lack of concentration while they are driving, particularly in areas where they are known, around home or school. At an early stage they have a fear of being seen by friends but as they become more accomplished they lose this fear and it gives way sometimes to life threatening waves to school pals.

"*What a bargain!*"

On the whole though, there's not a lot to choose between the sexes while they are learning. After the test is passed though it can be quite different.

I'll be accused of being sexist but, from my experience, men make better serious drivers than woman. There will be exceptions but when it comes to driving 30,000 plus miles a year, men have the edge. Large mileages require periods of intense concentration. Motorway driving can be arduous and tiring and although many of them are guilty of stupid behaviour at times, I feel men are better equipped to perform in this way, day after day.

There is a category of 'Expert drivers'. These are people who will have passed any driving test devised and will have driven almost anything on wheels. They will have taken part in competitions and rallies. Driving is in their blood and they form a very select club. They are often used by manufacturers to test new models and by companies who want to raise the standard of their drivers.

.. 🗓 ..

Bert is a retired A.D.I. who in an earlier period of his life occupied the air-gunner's seat in Lancaster bombers during the Second World War. He was one of the few brave souls who managed to complete 30 missions over enemy territory. During that time, as you'd imagine, he had many hairy moments in the air. He recorded some of them in a book which I've read and found very evocative.

In the 30 odd years he's been teaching people to drive, he has also had many hairy moments and probably because they are more recent than his flying escapades, he thinks that, the 'friendly fire' he has come under from other motorists, has posed more of a threat to his existence than all the flak the Germans aimed at his aircraft.

The point being I suppose, is that the German fighter pilots and gunners were fighting for their future, whilst the rushing motorist of later years if merely wanting to get past in order to pour a G & T down his neck that much sooner.

Three tales he recounted to me illustrate the good the bad and the couldn't care less attitude of three different examiners. Only one of them is currently working for the D.S.A.

Bert was giving a lesson when they came upon a stationary car with a man, who Bert recognised as an examiner, leaning in through the driver's open door. Bert asked his pupil to stop and he went to see what the matter was. It appeared that the candidate had fainted during the test. The examiner had used the dual controls to bring the car in towards the kerb and was now giving the man First-aid. Exactly what he was doing wasn't clear to Bert but it worked and the man recovered. Under the circumstances the examiner felt he was obliged to drive the car back to the test centre and return it to the waiting instructor. The test had to be terminated but the unfortunate candidate was alright, it appears he simply got over-stressed.

Another fainting candidate was a lady, who after being told she had failed her test, blacked out. This time however the examiner got out of the car and disappeared into the waiting room and then to his office on the first floor. The lady's instructor strolled back to the car and found his pupil slumped over the steering wheel. Failed candidates sometimes adopt this position so he didn't worry at first but when she didn't respond to his request to move over so he could drive them back, he realised something was amiss. He lifted her head, felt for her pulse and guessed what had happened. About this time the examiner's conscience must have bothered him, a window opened on the first floor and he called out rather weakly, "is she alright?"

"I think she will live but we had better have an ambulance"

The ambulance arrived, by this time the lady was conscious but they took her to hospital for a check up. It then fell to the A.D.I. to explain to the lady's husband what had happened. While he was telling him what had occurred he noticed the man becoming more and more agitated and as he finished giving him the details, the husband could contain himself no longer,

"Yes, yes but did she pass and is the car alright?"

The third of Bert's tales involved an A.D.I. who, having had his car serviced that morning, presented a pupil for test in the afternoon. He had the pre-test hour with his pupil and they parked outside the test centre at the appointed time. The examiner and candidate left for the test. Five minutes later the examiner appeared back in the waiting room and presented the A.D.I. with his car keys saying, "the test is terminated, your car won't start"

"I've only had it serviced this morning"

"Well it won't start now so the test is off".

Exit the A.D.I. from the waiting room, quick dash to the car.

"Switch on" he asked his pupil. Noise came from the starter motor but the engine refused to start. Bonnet up, the oil filter cap was missing but there was no oil splashed over the engine so it must have been on during their pre-test hour. Then he saw it lying across the points effectively shorting everything out and preventing the engine from staring.

He put the cap back in its rightful position and asked his pupil to switch on. Music to the ears. He made a quick dash back to the test centre, knocked on the examiner's door and explained what had happened but even though the whole incident hadn't taken more than eight minutes, the examiner refused to even consider taking the test.

"It wouldn't start so I've terminated the test and I'm just doing the paperwork now"

I'm sure most examiners now would be more understanding. Needless to say, some mechanic at a certain garage would get it in the neck for not putting the cap on correctly after filling the oil sump.

A Company I used to work for was Danish. I lived in Leeds and for most of my time with the Company I had an office in Rotherham, about 30 miles away.
A party of Danish directors made a flying visit on one occasion. After visiting the Rotherham branch it was their intention to move on and look round the Leeds branch. As it was the first time most of them had seen anything of the British side of their business they didn't know how to get from one to the other. I was delegated to be navigator as the Managing Director had to get back to the office - at least that is what he told me.

When they were ready to go, I brought my Cavalier from the car-park to the front of the office and took my place at the head of a little convoy of two black Mercedes and one black Granada.

We set off and headed north up the A1. All was well, until about 20 minutes later I looked at my fuel gauge, I was almost on fumes! A filling station was ahead at the top of the long hill. By holding my breath, I made it. I signalled left and pulled into the station, assuming that the 'convoy' would read the situation and carry on, expecting me to catch up with them when I'd re-fuelled. After all, these men were the brains of the Company....or were they?

As I pulled up by a pump, I looked behind me. In a long line, at this little filling station, which hadn't even gone self-service, was a Cavalier, two Mercedes and a Granada. The owner thought Christmas had come early. He rushed out, I was first in line so he said

"How many Sir?"

"Two gallons please, I'm in a hurry"

"No problem Sir"

It wasn't, I paid him, asked for a receipt, got in the car. He stood back as I pulled away and his chin must have hit the floor when he saw the last of the big spenders leaving his forecourt - followed by two big black Mercedes and a big black Granada!

Almost every year my wife and I take our holidays in Southern France. The roads are a delight to motor on and away from the large cities they are usually very quiet and uncrowded. Because we dislike ferries only slightly less than long tunnels we always take the short crossing from Dover to Calais. This means we have used the Port of Dover on many occasions.

During the writing of these notes it came time to make our annual pilgrimage to the land of frog's legs, snails and baguettes - only one of which we have a liking for. So it was that we entered the Port Authority's premises again. Something happened on this occasion that hadn't happened before.

The problem with only visiting such places once a year means that if changes have taken place you are quite probably unaware of them.

We made our lone approach to the small office which is manned by the port official who usually looks at our tickets, issues us with a windscreen sticker which says where we are going and then tells us which lane we must line up in after we have passed through at least two acres of wide open dockland and been waved and pointed at by half a dozen more officials, all usually with walkie-talkies glued to one ear.

As we neared his office, an arm appeared out of the window and waved towards us. I took this to mean, 'pass through', so I did, thinking they must have moved the check-in point further along. I thought - only thought - I heard a whistle, so I checked in my mirror. This served to confirm my actions as the disembodied arm was still waving. So on I went for about 100 metres, when a slip of a girl risked life and limb by leaping out in front of me, arm raised aloft. She unscrambled a walkie-talkie from her ear and looked at me through my open window with a mixture of sympathy and disdain on her face.

"You haven't checked in," she said, sounding like a junior Margaret Thatcher and gazing fixedly at the word 'Idiot' that was apparently tattooed across my forehead.

"He waved me on" said I, sounding like a *junior* Civil Servant.

147

"You'll have to go out and come back in again"

"Can't I just back up?"

"Against the rules, we can't have people reversing all over the place"

"I don't want to - - "

"Put this on your interior mirror, turn sharp right here and follow the 'Exit' signs. Go out of the port, round the roundabout and come back in again and this time stop at the check-in office"

She gave me a circular card which I hung on my mirror. I didn't look at it because I just knew it would say 'Idiot Card' in large Day Glo letters. I did my right-angle turn and found the first 'Exit' sign, that was easy because, bless her, she'd pointed it out to me. The second one was dead ahead and the third came shortly after but - isn't it always the same? - some schmuck had pinched the next one!

I wandered around looking for another 'Exit' notice but all I found was a long queue of very long lorries. I had hotel bookings which were dependent on me being on the ferry that day so, I turned away from the lorries to the left. Not a good idea. We soon came upon a brick wall. I used all my skill as an A.D.I. and completed a 7 point turn and there in front of me was a walkie-talkie with a man attached to it.

He looked as though he was about to tell me something that I already knew, 'I shouldn't be here,' when he spotted my 'Idiot' card dangling from my mirror.
Sympathy spread across his features and he very nicely asked me to follow him. He walked in front and took me across some bumps, I think they were cables, he came round to my window

and was about to say something when his walkie-talkie squawked. He thrust it to his ear with his left hand and pointed vaguely to his right. Crikey, I'm on my own again! I followed his pointing fingers, experiencing the same uneasy feeling I get going through the green door at the Customs. A motor cyclist passed me and I had a feeling of empathy with him, was this another 'Idiot'?

We turned a corner and there was the exit. Sinisterly there was a police car parked side ways on at the side of the exit facing us as we went out. I followed the motor cyclist round the roundabout just outside the docks and back in again towards the check-in office. I was right, the motor cyclist must have been another 'Idiot' because he pulled up and handed over his documents and was waved through within a minute or two.

I moved up and handed over my tickets. I enquired why I'd been waved through earlier. He denied waving me through but did say he had started to wave me back but realising I had gone too far he called up his travel agent to send me on a tour of the docks. I couldn't argue with him but I'm sure I saw a hand wave me through. He couldn't have been keeping his little helper on her toes could he?

.. 🕮 ..

I'm a non-smoker and since a minor nose operation some time ago, I have no sense of smell.

Carol was a heavy smoker and although I couldn't smell the tobacco, I knew it clung to her because my throat constricted and became quite sore for a while after her lessons. Apart from this discomfort her lessons proceeded without a hitch. I would pick her up from work in the City during her lunch break twice a week. She would come out of her office, light up a King Size, walk 20 metres to the car, drop it on the ground, stamp it out and another coffin nail bit the dust.

Carol told me she smoked to calm her nerves before her lessons but the stains on her fingers suggested she had been smoking much longer than she had even considered driving. Before her test she was like an unset jelly. We parked up half way through her pre-test hour so that she could light up and stamp out yet another King Size. At the test centre she lit up again, this girl was a serious smoker.

She went on test and I watched her come back. As I passed the examiner in the street, he said quite cheerfully, "I was worried about your car on a couple of occasions there." Gulp!
Carol was already out of the car and on fire.

"Where's your sheet?"

"On the seat" She said rhythmically.

I sat behind the steering wheel and looked at her driving test report. I was horrified. When a candidate fails, there will be usually a couple of crosses denoting the serious problems and there can be a fair few minor slashes where less problematic mistakes have been made.
Carol's sheet looked as though a duck with muddy feet had walked all over it. I didn't even bother to count her mistakes.

"I know I blew it but is that a bad report?" she asked through the window.

I asked her to do her war dance on her fag end and get in. As she did, I asked her if she had a ball-point pen in her hand bag. She found a Bic and gave me it asking why I wanted it. I put it behind my ear, "it's for the examiner next time I see him, it looks as though he used his up on your sheet."

"That bad then," she guessed.

During lessons she could drive perfectly well so, despite her horrible test result, I could not deny her the right to try again. Her second test came three weeks after the first one. So, three lessons and 30 packs of cigarettes later, we were up at the test centre again.

This time she passed with only three slashes against her. I have no explanation.

Having no sense of smell caused me acute embarrassment once.

I picked a young girl up from school for her lessons. I was a few minutes early on one occasion so I got out and dusted my windows while waiting. Sheila arrived and we got on with the lesson at the end of which, after she had got out, I set about doing the only bit of exercise I do these days. This consists of moving from the nearside seat to the offside seat by lifting myself over the gear lever and flopping into position behind the wheel.

I set off for my next pupil and as the song says, 'She was waiting at the gate'. For the second time in 10 minutes I did my bit of circuit training, vacating the driving seat for the passenger seat.

As my pupil opened the door to get in, she recoiled, "What's that awful smell?"

"What awful smell?" I asked innocently

"Look at your carpet"

I did, in fact I looked at both of them. It wouldn't be true to say they were *covered* but they both had a liberal serving of very pongy doggy doo on them. Fortunately they were both loose carpets and I could take them out and lob them in a nearby skip. My pupil couldn't believe I had been impervious to the smell.

Obviously when doing my spring cleaning, whilst waiting for Sheila, I'd picked it up on my shoes from the grass verge and transferred it from one side to the other while doing my aerobics. But how come Sheila hadn't noticed?

"Well I did but I didn't like to mention it," she told me at her next lesson. That innocence of youth caused me to have my windows down for a couple of days and to enquire of each pupil during that time if the car smelled alright.

I always ask to see my pupil's test appointment cards. After entering the date of the test in my appointment book, I will then hand the card back to the pupil. This has always been my policy as I am sure is the case with most A.D.I.'s. The need to do this was brought home to me about a year after I qualified.

A student came to me for lessons, with a test already booked. He'd had quite a number of lessons with another driving school but for whatever reason, he decided upon a change of instructor 6 weeks before his test.

"Let me see your appointment card Fred"

"I haven't got it with me but I will fetch it for you next lesson"

This conversation went on as the weeks went past.

Two weeks to go and although he was certain about the date, all he'd given me was a hazy estimate of the time. I gave him the test times on either side of the time he thought he was scheduled for. He called me that evening and confirmed his time. It went in my book. The next lesson arrived but still no card to settle any doubts in my mind as to whether he'd given me the correct one or just guessed it, so I gave him a phone number to call for confirmation. I didn't hear from him so I could only presume he had got it right.

We arrived at the test centre a couple of minutes before the appointed hour and waited. Examiners came and went with their candidates but on-one, it appeared wanted Fred. As the Senior Examiner was leaving I questioned him about Fred's appointment.

"You should have been here for the last test lad, you cost me 10p"

As they couldn't fit him in for the next test, which was the last one that day, he missed out.

Not only had he lost his appointment card he had also lost the sheet of paper with the phone number I had given him to ring up and find out what time his test was. Call it stupidity or simply a lack of concentration, whatever, it cost him the possibility of a driving licence and made me appear unprofessional. He left for Turkey within a week on a year's exchange visit. I bet he got lost.

I taught an Italian chef to drive. He worked in a local restaurant and I don't think we stopped laughing from start to finish. He didn't have the greatest command of English and my Italian stopped at Lefto and Righto. He'd done some driving in Italy and was a bit of a natural.

His girlfriend followed, she was South African of Italian parents. Her English was better than mine and with her clipped South African twang she made English sound very attractive. She worked as the receptionist at the restaurant and after they both passed they invited my wife and I to be their guests for an evening meal. It was very generous of them but we declined. They were saving up to get married and move to South Africa where they hoped, with her father's help, to open a restaurant of their own.

They seemed to be a generous crowd there. I subsequently taught a waiter and he celebrated by giving me a bottle of Moet & Chandon, which I *didn't* refuse. Cheers !

Paul should never have worn jeans but he wore them all the time. Jeans and check shirts, that was his 'uniform'. He was 33 and a Country and Western freak (his description, not mine) the reason he should have worshipped some other form of music that would allow him to wear something different, was his build. He was about 5'6" tall and about the same round his middle!

At the end of his lessons he had to get out of the car in order to extricate money from his pocket. My fees were £15 at the time and he always paid with a 5 and a £10 note. Most pupils sweat somewhat during their lessons but in Paul's case even his perspiration sweated. I could have made papier mache models out of the notes he gave me. After a couple of lessons I asked him to pay me at the start.

Paul lived half way up a narrow street that had a steep gradient. Going uphill he lived on the left. He had one lesson a week and we made good progress. As soon as he was capable he ended his lessons at home. The first time he did this I brought him downhill to his house as this was the easier approach and it showed him how to park on the 'wrong side' of the road. For a narrow street the cambers were quite steep and when he opened the door he lost hold of it and it swung away from him sharply. This was caused by a combination of the slope of the road, the sharp camber and a slight breeze. He apologised as the door jerked to a stop saying that the street was like a wind tunnel even with a breeze.

I made a mental note to come uphill in future and this we did at the end of his next lesson. I told him to push the door wide enough for it to hold itself open and he started to extricate himself. He was now getting out, uphill on two planes, against the slope of both the hill and the camber. He was definitely not a picture of elegance getting out of cars and the zip on his jeans couldn't take the strain. It split, fortunately Paul's underpants held and managed to preserve some of his dignity.

We simply had to come home downhill from then on. The one occasion we couldn't because of road works, I refused his offer to drop him at the bottom of the street and got him to drive up the hill. He parked up perfectly and to his relief, I helped him out of the car.

Test day came, it was a level road with not much of a camber. We parked up, had a chat, he was quite calm and confident. The time came to go into the waiting room, I got out of my side and

left him to do the same at his. As I shut my door I heard Paul's anguished cry,
"John, my zip's gone again."

I went round to survey the damage and he appeared to be intact.

"No it hasn't," I told him.

He'd shut the car door and was feeling for his zip. "Something's gone, I felt it go."

I peered into the uncharted territory between his legs and his jeans had come apart at the crotch. His double gusset had given way under the strain.

It wasn't a problem while he was standing or walking but when he sat down, his underpants would be on parade, always supposing they were holding up.

"You'll have to cross your legs when you sit down in the waiting room."

"I can't cross my legs."

"Oh come on Paul, I'm sure I've seen Johnny Cash cross his legs on a chat show."

"You probably have but his legs aren't as fat as mine."

It would have been cruel to have said the obvious, so I settled for, "O.K. we'll stand outside the waiting room until your examiner calls for you."

Normally this test centre is staffed by men but there was a lady examiner doing holiday relief that week, she'd taken one of my pupils the day before. Wouldn't you know, 'Sod's Law', Paul's name was called out by our lady. This worried me a bit because I didn't know the state of Paul's underpants - it's not something you spend a lot of time investigating on a busy street and I certainly wasn't going to do it in the privacy of the car. I was a little more tense than usual during the test.

I watched them leave and I watched them come back. She was smiling when she got out of the car and walked up the street towards the test centre. "Why the smile?" I wondered.

"Very nice drive that," she said.

"Oh, that's good, did he tell you about his jeans?"

"No, Why?"

"They came apart at the seams as he got out of the car and I was a bit worried what might happen when he turned round during his reverse manoeuvres."

"Well it was a bit of a struggle for him but he managed very well and nothing unexpected happened. Probably as well, it might have put me off sausages for life!"

My terms and conditions, a copy of which is given and explained to pupils at the start of a course of lessons, state that a minimum of 24 hours' notice is required to cancel a lesson without the loss of the fee for it. This is not very demanding and most driving schools, whether or not they would enforce it, would require longer.

If I am not given sufficient notice I would use my discretion whether to ask for the lesson fee. Fortunately I don't have to worry too much about this aspect as I don't get many short notice cancellations. When they do occur, the attitude of the pupil can differ wildly.

Young mums can find it a problem if illness strikes the family suddenly and they are very apologetic and I've known them offer to pay for the lesson. Others can be totally different. One superior type came to the door in his dressing gown, at 11 o'clock in the morning, looked a bit startled and said, "sorry old boy, I've got a dental appointment in half an hour, we'll have to cancel our lesson."

"Why didn't you ring me?"

"Only found the dentist's card this morning."

"Well I'm sorry but I will have to charge you for the lesson."

"Why is that? Can't we just re-arrange for next week?"

Well-off parents are equally 'innocent' in this respect. Occasionally I have known them want to cancel a lesson when I've got to their doorstep, because Willie or Susie has too much homework to do. "But he'll be alright for next week"

No offer to pay for the lesson is usually forthcoming, so when the subject is broached, a fit of the vapours follows. Why can't they realise that an hour of my time booked as a lesson constitutes a contract? If I hadn't 'sold' them that hour, I would most likely have sold it to someone else.

It is the attitude of the person involved that makes me decide whether to charge or not.

Taken to it's logical conclusion, if I do charge, it is purely for the inconvenience caused or as an attempt to stop any future thoughtless actions taking place. The cancelled lesson will take place at a later date, any pupil is going to require a certain number of lessons to become test ready, therefore cancelling any lessons only stretches the course out over a longer period of time and causes no eventual financial hardship to A.D.I.'s. So a phone call in time could prevent a wasted journey and could result in a cup of tea as a welcome break and pleasant relations being sustained.

Common sense and intelligence don't always go hand in hand. I suppose it's unfair to generalise but I have found that really intelligent people can find it difficult to pick up the basics of driving, simply because they appear to have a need to analyse things too much, early on. Details can be added later when they will be easier to digest. People who rely on common sense to see them through life adapt to driving better because they are more willing to take things one step at a time.

I have taught six doctors to drive and many nurses. I don't want any nurse to start beating me on the head with a big stick, my inferences are meant to be complementary, when I say that I have never had any trouble teaching them - but the doctors gave me a few problems by being mainly impatient.

One foreign doctor called me saying she had an International Driving Permit and she wanted to obtain a British driving licence. On her first lesson I asked to see her international permit and found it was three months out of date. Some countries have an agreement whereby a British licence can be issued on the strength of a licence obtained in the home country. This lady didn't come from such a country. She had driven to meet me, illegally it seemed.

I asked her if she had applied for a provisional licence. "No I'm driving on my international licence."

"But that's out of date."

"What must I do then?"

"Apply for a provisional, put 'L' plates on your car and don't drive unless you're accompanied by a qualified driver."

"You're joking."

I assured her I was not and further disappointed her by saying we couldn't start lessons until she had her provisional licence.

As this would probably take two weeks to arrive, assuming she applied immediately, I could only book her in and watch her drive home, illegally.

I started picking her up, after she obtained her provisional, from her home in the Hospital grounds. Her car was often in a different position when I called for her but it never had 'L' plates on it. She let it slip that she was still driving on her own, despite my warning her that she would be invalidating her insurance, and that it could be very serious if she was involved in an accident.

Remember, the following came from the mouth of a doctor...
"I've got my international licence so I might as well use it and if I get stopped, I'll plead ignorance."

Chapter Ten
FINALLY........

Early on in my career as a driving instructor, a Leeds publican asked me for lessons. He'd had about 15 hours instruction from two A.D.I..'s already. He was in his 30's and although a bit forceful changing gear, he wasn't too bad.

By the third lesson however his concentration appeared to start wandering. He seemed more interested in what we were passing than where we were going. At the start of his fourth and fifth lessons he actually asked if we could conduct them in a certain suburb of Leeds. No problem, it was an area I often used for lessons. He told me by way of explanation that he might be buying a house in that area in order to get away from the pub after hours.

The next lesson, he wanted to call in at a branch of his bank on the outskirts of Leeds and also to visit a record shop opposite the bank. He was out of the car 20 minutes doing these chores. I pointed out that he was missing a large chunk of his lesson by his actions.

"No problem."

Next lesson he asked to go to the suburb where we had been two lessons earlier and visit an estate agent. The penny dropped. He was doubling up my use as an instructor with his version of a taxi service.

What do I do? Sit tight and just take an hour's fee for about 40 minutes work or protest that I am not being allowed to do my job properly by allowing myself to be drawn into these excursions?

I put my problem to him and of course *he* didn't see it as a problem.

"I'm quite content to pay you for what we're doing and of course, I'm learning to drive at the same time as getting a number of jobs done that would cost more by taxi or take an age by bus."

He had a point but it still didn't seem right, if for no other reason than that some of my best friends are taxi drivers.

As it turned out, I wasn't the only one worrying about his behaviour. He was sacked by the brewery two weeks after our discussion for neglecting the pub.

So, as my pupils often say, I should stop worrying. His lessons came to an abrupt end.

Sometime later the publican's son came to me for lessons and I was to find out that his misdemeanours at the pub had not only cost him his job but his marriage had ended because of it.

His son had been at school with the first boy I had taught to drive - the one I'd exchanged High 5's with in the middle of the road afterwards. I was given the shocking news that he had died in a car accident about two years afterwards. Naturally I was affected by this news and the thought was with me for a long time.

Seven years later I received a phone call. It rather stunned me because it came from someone I had been told, on good authority, was dead. It was my ex-pupil who was supposed to have died in a car accident, he wanted me to give lessons to a friend of his. He looked remarkable well for someone who'd been dead this past 8 or 9 years and I never did find out how the mistake had come about - because it doesn't seem right to say to someone in his 20's: "I thought you <u>was</u> dead and buried!"

Learner drivers on the motorway system has long been a contentious issue. At present it is necessary to have passed a practical driving test before being allowed onto the motorway. The moment that test is passed, a new driver can go on the motorway and for the first time in their life, in all probability, drive at 70 miles an hour in any sort of weather conditions and in amongst the fast moving assorted traffic.

I'm not saying they *will* do and the sensible ones will most likely have reservations about doing so but some will decide to go for a 'burn' simply for the sensation.

How much safer, for everyone concerned, if this sensation could be had, before taking the practical test, under the supervision of an A.D.I. in a vehicle with dual controls? Very few drivers return to their instructor, after passing their test, for a motorway lesson. Speeds on this type of road can be very deceptive, including that of the vehicle you are driving.

I had a pupil for a motorway lesson and she was ploughing along merrily when I asked her if she was aware of her speed.

"Good God, I'm doing 84!"

Then she howled, "John, the brakes won't work."

The brake wouldn't work because my foot was on its side under my dual brake in order to stop her banging her foot down when she realised the speed she was travelling at.

"Have you checked your mirror, Bev?"

She did then and saw a lorry about 30 metres behind us. That lorry could have made quite an impression on our rear end if Bev had whacked the brake on.

This perfectly true, and probably common event, reiterates my belief that learner drivers would benefit from some properly controlled, pre-test motorway experience. If Bev had been on her own on the motorway for the first time and having been worried by her speed, would she have remembered her mirror check before applying the brake? The lorry might not have hit her but what might have been happening behind the lorry when the driver went for his brakes? Could there be another vehicle behind and another and another?

During lessons we teach pupils to use mirrors in the normal course of driving and especially at certain times. How many of us can say we are faultless in the use of mirrors? If experienced drivers can forget to make a necessary check, how can we expect even a properly trained new driver, to remember this important point every time, especially when under pressure?

The following tit bit could possibly save the Government millions of pounds in road building costs and spare the public the advent of Toll Roads. It would cut out a lot of pollution and in time, return the British Isles to the quiet little backwater it was between the two World Wars.

The extended Theory Test, which came onto the statute books as of 1st July 1996, has had a remarkable effect on the number of people taking practical driving tests. It has had a corresponding effect on the number coming for driving lessons.

The Theory Test has to be passed before a Practical Test can be applied for. It consists of 35 multi-choice questions of which, originally, 26 had to be answered correctly. This proved to be too easy, only 9 or 10 out of every 100 candidate were failing. Results like that must mean that the test had not been set properly to examine the participants and besides the D.S.A. was missing out on re-test fees.

So, three months after it was introduced, we found the goalposts being moved. The pass mark was raised to 30, this had the effect of causing around 40 out of every 100 to fail. More like a test now and the extra revenue must have paid a few bills for the D.S.A..

To get back to my original point, if this test had been introduced years ago, we wouldn't have so many vehicles on the road because there wouldn't have been the drivers to drive 'em. The fact that so many are failing the Theory Test is putting many, many, more off going in for a driving licence.

So, the solution to any future over-crowding on our roads is simple, make the Theory pass rate 35 out of 35. It will bankrupt a lot of driving instructors, car sales will slump, examiners will be laid off, revenue from fuel oils and road tax will diminish. Garages and the spare parts industry will suffer - but not to worry. As existing drivers die off, the rest of us will be able to get where we want to be without any traffic jams - that's if we can afford the inflated prices for fuel and tax.

On the other hand — Government could realise that this is not a good scenario and instead of thinking of ways to make it more difficult to pass the Theory Test, they might consider its long term effect and whether it really does have any bearing on road safety. Because the Test is more difficult to pass than the older type of Highway Code session in the car, it is making candidates swot up more beforehand - but are they retaining the knowledge? During a motorway lesson, I posed 15 questions to a student who had passed her Theory Test 6 weeks previously. She failed to answer more than three with any degree of certainty. She wasn't driving at the time, we'd pulled into a service area for that specific purpose.

If drivers don't remember the content, what good is it when all they are doing is swot for the test? Especially if the spin-off is that so many people are being put off taking up driving because of it.

Solution? There is no way the Theory Test can be scrapped but if the pass rate were to be reduced to 28 we would have more passes, at no detriment to road safety and many more people would be attracted back into having a go. Lost re-test fees would be made up from the extra people taking the test . 26 to 30 was too big a jump particularly when the goal-posts were moved again and the question bank was enlarged.

Youngsters wanting to start lessons on or soon after their 17th Birthday must make sure they have their provisional licence available at the time. This means they must send off for it a few weeks before their birthday. It's always as well, particularly with the very young looking ones, for A.D.I.'s to check that they have *indeed* reached their Birthday by opening up the licence and checking with their date of birth which is printed on it.

With older pupils this isn't necessary, we'd make sure the licence is signed and hand it back to them.

When I picked Imran up to start lessons he hadn't signed his licence. I gave him a pen and he signed and put his licence in his shirt pocket. He'd be about 22 or 23, no need to check his birth date. He'd been in and out of cars all his life, his two elder brothers worked for a Private Hire Car Company and Imran told me, he fitted in working on the radio at the Hire Company's office, with his hotel management course at college. He picked driving up quite quickly and at two lessons a week he made good progress.

He told me on his 8th lesson that he was getting married in 4 weeks time on his birthday.

"That sounds a good idea, how old will you be?"

"17."

"Sorry?"

"17."

"Er - pull up on the left."

He did.

"How old will you be in 4 weeks time?"
"17."

"Can I see your driver's licence?"

I unfolded his licence hoping that this was some form of 'Ethnic' joke. It wasn't. He was 16 and 11 months and for one of those months I had been teaching him to drive. For God's sake, on Friday he would be clean shaven and by Tuesday he had got a beard. I go away on holiday for two weeks and don't shave, when I get back no-one notices. He gets more hair on his chin in 4 days than I've got on my head and he's not yet 17!

So we suspended lessons for 6 weeks, 4 for him to reach 17 and the other two for him to get over his wedding.

Normal service resumed after that, he convinced me he didn't know he had been in the wrong. The innocent way he had brought the subject up proved it to me and I didn't question him as to whether his brothers' knew the law in that respect. After a further dozen or so lessons he was good enough for his test which he failed and he was to fail 4 more before he passed at his 6th attempt.

This lad was a good driver who just couldn't hold himself together on test. I sat in on his 4th and 5th and couldn't believe it was the same driver who had done everything right the hour before. After his 5th test he took a three month sabbatical.

Before his 6th test he had 5 lessons and passed. When I dropped him at home, one of his brothers was waiting for him. On being told by Imran that he had passed, his brother said,
"Good , you're legal tonight."

On questioning, I found that, during his three month break, he had been driving private hire cars.

Until I got bored with the colour, I had a succession of red cars, always Renaults. When I bought my present model I decided on a change.

Cars are not red or blue now are they? The colour always has to have an additional word in front of it to personalise the colour to specific manufacturers. I thought I was getting a 'dark blue' as a change from 'red'. Don't be silly, 'dark blue' is too common, it's 'Stratos Blue'. Was it Henry Ford who kept things nice and simple by saying you can have one of my cars in any colour you choose so long as it's black? I'm told that nowadays there are many shades of black.

One day while driving a red car, sorry, that should be 'carmine' red, I ended up with a face to match.

I arrived to pick a 17 year old boy up for his first lesson. He'd wanted a two hour lesson but I had not been able to give him two consecutive hours so he was having a split with two hours in between.

He came out without his provisional so I sent him back in for it. After about 5 minutes his dad came out to tell me Philip was having difficulty locating his licence. He started talking about cars and asked what I thought about Renaults and seemed interested when I told him how reliable I found them. He drove a Peugeot which had never let him down. Philip came out clutching his unsigned provisional and we set off for our first hour.

As happens so often during a first lesson Philip stalled the car. No problem I told him and explained what he had done wrong. After a while I asked him to switch on, he did but not a lot happened. My battery was flat, it needed topping up. The upshot of this was Philip, on his first lesson had the pleasure of pushing me for a bump start. The lesson finished without any similar mishaps and I dropped him off.

I should have gone into a garage and topped up straight away but I forgot, as simple as that, I forgot. The next two pupils were experienced and their lessons went off, without a hitch.

I picked Philip up for his second hour and things went swimmingly until very near the end he let the clutch up too quickly and we stalled. For the second time in a day, he had to give me a shove. Lesson over I took him home and made arrangements for the following week.

When I picked him up, he gave me a note from his Dad, it just said, 'Buy Peugeot.' Serves me right for opening my big mouth.

This will sound familiar to a lot of people.

"It was awful," she said, "I had to go on roads I'd never been on before. The car stalled itself at a busy junction and this bus suddenly pulled away from a bus-stop without signalling. That made the car stall again. Why do cars do that? Why do they always stall at awkward moments? Then I'd to go on some more strange roads, tight bends, junctions, parked cars, pedestrians all over the place, it was awful. I never ever want to do that again"

Was this a candidate who'd just failed her test? NO — it was my wife looking for a filling station.

As a parent, I know I would have worried had I been told, by either of my sons' driving instructors, "well he's passed his test but he has a habit of driving much too fast unless I'm continually on at him to slow down".

Nowadays there are even more things to worry about when teenagers are growing up than there were when my two were in that age bracket. I've spoken about this with other A.D.I.'s on a number of occasions. A long-time instructor once told me, in relation to this issue, "we're paid to teach 'em to drive not how to live their lives. Leave that to their parents".

Fair enough, but if we know something as important as this 'speed factor' undoubtedly is, shouldn't we inform the parents?

On reflection, had it been a problem with my lads, I would have appreciated being told - despite the obvious worry it would have caused. I could then have travelled with them more often that I might otherwise have done until I was satisfied they were settling down and driving steadily.

This thought prompts me to have a word with parents if I feel there is a justifiable need and suggest that they accompany their youngsters until *they* too are satisfied.

For the more mature speed merchants and I use the word 'mature' cautiously, I have an A4 sheet of paper which depicts in horrific detail a split second breakdown of what happens to both car and driver should they be unfortunate enough to run into a tree at 55mph.

We teach them, examiners pass them and from then on, it's down to common sense and hopefully guidance from people around them.

We were on our way to the test centre, the pre-test hour had gone smoothly, confidence was as good as could be expected, 10 minutes before his appointed meeting with destiny.

A red traffic light was holding up our progress at a major junction. The traffic coming across us had stopped so our light was about to change. He moved smoothly into first gear, hand on handbrake.

From a chemist's shop on our left emerged a <u>very</u> large lady. Seeing the row of stationary cars, she started to run for the pedestrian crossing immediately in front of our car. This lady wasn't built for running, it was summer and underneath her bright summer dress there was a lot of movement. Red and amber had appeared as she dashed in front of us.

She appeared to wave her thanks as she passed. I remember thinking that, if her dress had been waterproof, it would have made a good cover from my car and I had this mental picture of a couple of ferrets fighting in a sack as she reached the other pavement.

The sound of a car horn brought us out of our reverie, the light was now green and my pupil moved through the junction and up the hill towards the test centre.

Thinking he might have been disturbed by the event I tried to put him at ease by making light of it, "how would you like to have to fight for the bed-clothes with her on a cold winter's night?"

"Not really, it was my wife's Auntie Pam."

Ooooops !!

.................and finally.

Driving Instructors are, in the main self employed men or women who choose to earn their living in what can be a very enjoyable profession.

They will by the nature of their work, experience a few hairy moments along the way, these will come to even the most vigilant of the species and will, more often than not, be caused by other drivers.

Some instructors have been doing the job all their working lives, while others will have come to it because grants were available to off-set training costs after redundancy forced them to leave other occupations.

However they arrived in driver training, I hope they enjoy it as much as I have done. Provided they take things as they come and laugh at the funny moments and don't get too uptight if things don't go according to plan, then I'm sure the laughs will make up for the frowns and the pleasure that comes when that seemingly impossible pupil passes a test is immeasurable.

Any views or opinions expressed within these pages are mine and do not necessarily agree with officialdom.